BOMBING IN BELGRAVIA

CASSIE COBURN MYSTERY #2

SAMANTHA SILVER

BLUEBERRY BOOKS PRESS

Copyright © 2021 by Samanatha Silver

All rights reserved.

No part of this book may be reproduced in any form or by any electronic or mechanical means, including information storage and retrieval systems, without written permission from the author, except for the use of brief quotations in a book review.

Cover design by ebooklaunch.com

❀ Created with Vellum

CHAPTER 1

I grabbed my buzzing phone off my nightstand, looked at the time, and groaned. One forty-six in the morning. Who in their right mind could *possibly* be calling me at this hour?

"Hurro?" I mumbled into the receiver unenthusiastically.

"'Allo, Cassie? There is a liver here I want you to look at," the voice on the other end said in a strong French accent. Of course. Only Violet Despuis would think that calling me in the middle of the night to look at a liver was an acceptable thing to do.

"Violet, it's the middle of the night."

"Yes, it is."

"I'm sleeping."

"This is far more interesting."

"It can wait until morning," I replied, closing my eyes and pressing the big red button on my screen to end the call. I put the phone back down on the nightstand and closed my eyes, ready to go back to sleep, when it buzzed to life again.

I sighed and stared at the ceiling. There really was no getting away from this, was there?

"It cannot wait until morning," Violet said as way of greeting when I picked up the phone again. "I need to know now."

"Need to know what?"

"If this person was killed in an explosion, or poisoned."

"What?"

"I need to know if this person was killed in an explosion, or if they were poisoned first."

"I heard you, I just can't believe that's the sentence I just heard."

"Well, it is. Now get up and come here."

"Fine," I muttered, rubbing the sleep out of my eyes and carefully getting out of bed so as to not disturb Biscuit, the little orange cat I'd taken in after his previous owner had been murdered. He looked so peaceful and warm, sleeping curled up in a little ball on top of my blanket. I wished I was still sleeping as well, but I was sure that Violet wasn't going to give up until I arrived at her crime scene.

Violet Despuis was… well, I wasn't quite sure what she was. She didn't work for the police, although she often helped them solve cases. She wasn't a traditional private investigator, but I supposed that must have been the closest thing to a job title that she had. She was French, she was eccentric, and she was an absolute genius.

I had run into Violet at a police station after my bike was stolen a month earlier. She had been investigating a series of poisonings, and decided to have me tag along with her after realizing I was suffering from depression. I'd just moved to London after an accident ended my promising career as a surgeon before it had even begun, in an attempt to get out of the depressive funk I'd been in for the previous ten months.

And now, instead of standing in a San Francisco operating room, fixing a soccer player's torn Achilles tendon, I was making my way through the streets of London just before three in the morning at the request of a woman I was fairly certain was certifiably insane, just to look at a liver.

EVEN THOUGH SLOANE SQUARE was only one tube station away from me on the Circle and District lines, unfortunately neither one of them had night services yet—the last train on both lines was just before one in the morning, and they would start again around four thirty—so I hailed a cab and five minutes later found myself at the address Violet had texted to me.

I still would have found the place even without the address. As the taxi made its way down Bourne Street, the brick walls of the row houses along the street were lit up in a cacophony of red and blue lights. Crowds of curious locals poked their heads out of windows to find out what was going on, while the more energetic among them made their way down the street toward where the action was.

I paid the cabbie and walked along with the others toward the gathering crowd. Bobbies in uniform lined a string of yellow police tape that blocked off an entire section of the street. As I pushed my way toward the front, I saw what had happened.

It looked like a whole house had exploded. Brown bricks were scattered across the road, mingled with white rendering that had come from the bottom of the house. A car parked in front of what had previously been a house had its windshield and passenger side window shattered, the rest of it covered in brick dust. The splintered remains of a black door had been blown so far that they were now leaning against the house on the other side of the street.

Police officers were putting up barriers to prevent the public from seeing anything. I suddenly spotted Violet and called out to her.

"Violet! Hey!" I said, waving a hand. She looked up and spotted me, then motioned me over. Of course, she looked like she'd just woken up after a nice, long rest. She wore skinny jeans and an oversized black and white striped shirt that hung off one shoulder, with a nice scarf wrapped around her long, brown hair that was tied back into a ponytail. I looked around for a second, and then ducked under the police ropetape.

"Excuse me, miss, you can't be over here," a policeman told me, but the next thing I knew Violet was next to me.

"She is with me. I have invited her," Violet said.

"Well she still can't be here," the man replied. "The fact that you're here is a travesty by itself."

"The fact that you are a grown man who believes a few strands of fuzz comprises a moustache is a travesty, but you do not see me preventing you from doing your work because of it," Violet snapped back, taking me by the arm and leading me past the man as he ran his finger over his upper lip anxiously.

"I am glad you came," Violet told me. "You must come and see this."

"What happened?" I asked as I looked at the carnage all around us.

"It was a gas explosion," Violet replied. "There are three victims. One is at the hospital, the other two are dead." We made our way past the first body, that of a man in his late twenties, maybe early thirties. He'd had black hair in life, and what I could see of his skin that wasn't covered in burns was olive-colored. One of his arms was missing. A medical examiner, a short man with graying hair, leaned over the body, while the flash of the police photographer's camera pierced the dark night at steady intervals.

Violet led me deeper into the heart of the explosion, toward the house.

"Why do you want me to look at a liver if this was just a gas explosion?" I asked Violet.

"Exactly," was all she replied, and I shook my head, confused. We gingerly walked up the steps into what had formerly been a beautiful home—Belgravia was one of the most expensive neighborhoods in London—and made our way into what had formerly been a living room.

Half a television was still mounted on the wall, wires protruding from the broken glass where the explosion had destroyed it. A leather couch covered in dust on the other side was where we found the body, lying prone. Her hair was as dark as the other man's, her skin the same color. The woman's dark eyes looked blankly at the ceiling. Her knees were curled up to her chest, as if she knew the explosion was coming and had gone into the fetal position to protect herself.

Violet walked up to the body and motioned me over. I made my way to her and had a look.

All around the body were shards of glass; I noticed that the coffee table in front of the couch was missing the glass top.

When I looked down at the body, it was obvious the glass had done a lot of damage. The girl's abdomen was sliced open.

"Have a look at the liver," Violet told me, handing

me a pair of latex gloves. I slipped them on and crouched down next to the body.

As soon as I glanced at the liver, I knew what Violet was looking at. Instead of being a rust-like red color, it was a deep yellow-orange color. I looked up at Violet and raised my eyebrows.

"Are there any regular reasons why a presumably healthy young woman would have a yellow liver?" Violet asked. "I must admit, there may be a regular explanation for this," she continued.

I shook my head. "No. Not that I can think of."

"Can you smell anything strange?" Violet asked. I leaned tentatively in toward the body and sniffed. The only thing I could smell was the brick dust, and natural gas. I leaned back and shook my head no.

"There is a smell there. It is difficult to notice through the other smells of the accident, but there is a garlic smell there."

"Garlic," I said to myself softly, thinking back through years and years of learning everything I could about medicine and the human body. Suddenly, it came to me. "Arsenic!" I exclaimed. "You think she was poisoned with arsenic."

"I do not think. I am certain of it. The scent of garlic confirms. If we were to look at the lining of the stomach, I expect it would be inflamed. But we do not need to do that. For now, we continue on the assumption that this woman did not die in a gas explosion. This woman was dead before it took place."

CHAPTER 2

"That's some pretty terrible luck, then," I said to Violet as I looked down at the victim. "To be poisoned and then blown up."

"It is not bad luck if the explosion was done to cover up the poisoning."

I looked at Violet, shocked. "Do you really think that's what happened?"

Violet shrugged. "I do not know anything. All I know for certain is that this girl was dead before the explosion, and likely not from natural causes. We have a theory; we theorize that the explosion was not an accident either. Now we find evidence to prove or disprove it."

I had to admit, despite the total lack of sleep and the fact that it was the middle of the night, I was curious. I followed Violet as she made her way toward a tall, authoritative looking woman in a dark blue shirt sporting a London fire brigade logo. She was speaking with another firefighter, and when she was finished she turned to us.

"Ah, Violet," she greeted warmly. "I'm glad to see you working on this case." She smiled at me and held out a hand.

"Laurie Summers. I'm the chief investigator here with the fire department."

"Cassie Coburn," I replied. "I'm a friend of Violet's, and, uh, I guess her walking medical encyclopedia and sounding board," I continued, earning a smile from the woman. Before she could reply though, Violet interrupted.

"So it is not an accidental explosion then?" Violet asked. "You say you are glad I am here. That means there is foul play involved."

"Oh yes, I think so," Laurie told us, motioning for us to follow her. "I can't be one hundred percent sure, but I'm reasonably certain," she said as she headed deeper into the house, into what obviously used to be the kitchen. "This here used to be an oven," she said, motioning to a lump of metal and plastic that was still reasonably identifiable, all things considered. "A gas oven, specifically."

Grunting, Laurie moved the oven aside, then motioned for us to look at the pipe fitting against the wall. It was a short piece of black tubing, with a gold tip that was covered in dust from the explosion.

"We found this like this," Laurie said.

"Ah," Violet nodded, and I tried to think about what it meant.

"So… the tubing is disconnected from the oven, and if it had been connected during the explosion, it wouldn't have come apart?" I attempted.

"*Exactement!*" Violet exclaimed happily.

"That's correct," Laurie confirmed, nodding. "There's only one thing I don't understand though; it's why the woman on the sofa didn't smell the leak. For there to have been enough gas to cause an explosion of this size, she must have smelt it. My best guess is she was having a nap."

"That one I can answer for you," Violet replied. "She was already dead. The woman on the sofa was killed before the explosion."

Laurie's mouth dropped open. "Seriously? Well yeah, I guess that's as good a reason as any to be unable to smell the leak."

"What is it that triggered the blast?" Violet asked.

"Our best guess right now is that the other victim entered the home and flicked the light switch. The spark caused the large amount of natural gas inside the home to ignite, hence the explosion."

"So the second victim knew the first victim well enough to simply enter the home on his own," Violet muttered, almost to herself.

"Of course, all of this is totally off the record," Laurie said. "I won't have a full report out for at least a week, in all likelihood. I also don't know whether there are any fingerprints on the tubing yet. I'm hoping we'll find some."

"Of course," Violet replied. "As you say. But as you know, I do not need official reports. I simply need the truth."

"Don't we all," Laurie replied, giving us a quick wave as Violet and I headed toward an official looking policeman.

"She seems nice," I said to Violet as we walked through the rubble.

"She is not only nice, she is good at her job. I am always happy when Laurie Summers is in charge of arson investigations. It always saves me time, as I do not need to do the fire brigade's job as well as the police's job."

I smiled to myself as we approached one of those very policemen. Violet had a very high opinion of herself; from all I had seen, she had every right to, but it was still a little bit strange to hear her brag so casually of her skills.

The policeman Violet was approaching, however, obviously didn't have the same opinion of her. I wasn't surprised. DCI Williams at the Paddington Green station seemed to be one of the few members of the Metropolitan Police Force who could actually stand Violet. This man was short and stout; he reminded me of the Fat Controller from Thomas the Tank Engine, only more scowly.

"Violet Despuis. Has no one told you this is a crime scene? What are you doing behind the yellow tape?"

"I'm investigating a murder, Inspector Chase."

"No, we, the police, are investigating a murder. You are a member of the public who isn't welcome here."

"Really? Can you tell me how the primary murder victim was killed?" Violet asked, and the man looked at her like she was a crazy person.

"Look around, how do you think?" he asked, motioning with his hands at the wreckage that surrounded us.

"So the police still believe the woman was killed in the explosion?"

"Of course she was," the man replied, getting visibly angry now. "Stop wasting my time."

"It is not me who is wasting your time," Violet replied. "If you look at the dead woman's liver, you will notice she was poisoned, most likely by arsenic, and was dead before the explosion took place. In fact, I believe the explosion was a clumsy attempt at hiding the murder."

The inspector's mouth dropped open for a split second before he took control of himself once more and closed it. "Stay here," he barked at us as he made his way to one of the crime scene investigators, with whom he had a few words, before the investigator moved toward the woman's body. He returned to the inspector a moment later, ashen faced and obviously abashed.

"Fine. You can stay. But *don't touch anything*," he admonished when he returned, around five minutes later. It seemed that the pathologist had missed the detail of the woman already being dead the first time he had looked her over.

"Oh yes, it is my first time at a crime scene, I really have no idea what I am doing," Violet replied, rolling her eyes. "Now, who are the victims?" she asked.

"The man in the hospital is Andrew Greenhouse. His wife says he was coming home from a late night at work; he lives about ten minutes from here. It looks like he was just in the wrong place at the wrong time. The two dead victims, we're not sure yet."

"Well, who does the house belong to?" The inspector shifted from foot to foot. Even I could tell he was visibly uncomfortable with where this conversation was going.

"A man called Lee Yang Lin," he replied.

Violet looked up. "Leo Lin?" she asked. "The UK's ambassador to Taiwan?"

The inspector nodded glumly.

"How can you *possibly* know that?" I said, mostly stunned. I came from the part of America with the greatest links to Asia, and yet I had absolutely no idea who the American ambassador to Taiwan was.

"It's my job to know these things," Violet replied. "Lin has two children, both attending the London School of Economics. Twins," she said, looking toward where the police officers were laying a sheet over the man.

"You can see why I don't want you involved in this case," the inspector said to Violet. "It's far too sensitive a situation."

"Yes, I will simply explain to the ambassador that his children's murder could have been solved far more quickly and efficiently than by a police force who didn't even realize his daughter had been poisoned, but that due to the sensitivity of the case, his children's murderer will remain free."

The inspector's face turned such a deep red that I began to wish there was an ambulance nearby in case his head actually exploded.

"You wouldn't dare," he hissed at Violet.

"You cannot prevent me from investigating anything. The two of us both know I am better at this job than your entire police force, so if you do not want to both humiliate your entire department and alienate the Taiwanese when you fail to find a killer, you will let me do what it is I do."

Violet's deep brown eyes were as hard as steel. When she wanted to work a case, she did *not* take no for an answer, no matter how much the police disliked having her around.

"Fine, but if you find the killer, you don't get any credit."

"When have I ever asked for credit when I do your

job?" Violet replied. "Let the morgue know I will be there in the morning."

With that, Violet turned on her heel and headed back toward the house. I followed her as she crouched down, looking at every little thing.

"You know, you could just leave this case alone," I told her. "The cops usually do manage to find the guilty party eventually."

"It is not about finding the guilty party," Violet told me. "It is more about the intrigue of the crime. And this crime, it has the intrigue. I believe that both of the Lin twins were targets of the crime. The way the perpetrator managed to kill them both took a lot of creativity, although the execution was not perfect."

"What do you mean?" I asked. "Only the girl was killed before the explosion."

"Yes, but how was the explosion supposed to happen?" Violet asked. "The person responsible leaked the gas, but they did not put a newspaper in the toaster and leave. They did not throw a Molotov cocktail into the home from afar. No, they leaked the gas, and then they waited for the brother to come home and turn on the light when he entered the home. They would have only done that if they knew the brother was coming home, and therefore, he was also a target of the crime."

"And so the goal was to make it look like the girl was on the couch, didn't notice the gas leak, and that when the brother came home he accidentally blew up the house?"

"*Exactement,*" Violet replied, nodding. "It was all supposed to look accidental. However, the explosion was not as large as the murderer must have hoped; we are able to tell that the girl was poisoned, and that the leak was done on purpose. Although the execution was not perfect, the idea behind the crime was inspired. Yes, this is a crime that I am very interested in solving. I do not believe the police will find it simple to solve. There is an intelligent mind at work behind this crime."

We spent a few more minutes at the crime scene before Violet hailed a cab and we headed back home.

CHAPTER 3

*V*iolet lived down the street from me; she had been the one to introduce me to my new landlady, Mrs. Michaels. The cab took us back to Violet's place, but before I could head back to my basement apartment under Mrs. Michaels' home, Violet motioned for me to follow her to her place.

It looked like that was all the sleep I was going to get tonight.

"Come and help me," Violet told me. "The last time, I worked well when I—how do you say— bounced ideas off you. I think with this case, it will be necessary for me to do that again."

"Ok," I replied, following her to her home. I had to admit, there was something thrilling about watching Violet try and solve crimes. And now that I'd seen the bodies, I was curious as to who had killed the ambassador's children.

We made our way into her study, right off the side of the front door. The whole room was lined with books, but Violet immediately made her way to the far corner, where she had a computer sitting on a desk. Violet sat in front of it as I pulled up a straight-backed chair that was surprisingly comfortable and watched as she typed in the name *Leo Lin* into Google.

Lee Yang Lin, who went by Leo most of the time, was born in London to parents who had emigrated from Taiwan in the late 1950s. They ran a dry cleaning business in central London, and when Leo graduated from high school at the top of his class, he was accepted into Oxford University, where he studied Law. He married a woman from Yorkshire and they had two children; a pair of fraternal twins named Jenny and Kevin. Going by the pictures we saw online, those were in fact the two victims of the explosion. Both were students at the London School of Economics— Jenny was working on her law degree while Kevin worked on his Master's degree in economics.

"Those were definitely our two victims," Violet said when we saw a picture of the twins together.

"Absolutely," I replied. "I wouldn't want to have to be the person to tell the parents that their only two children were killed tonight."

Wordlessly, Violet opened the Facebook pages for both victims. Jenny Lin's profile was filled with selfies, pictures with other students, business class plane trips to and from Taiwan and luxury handbags. She was well and truly living the dream life of the rich university student.

Kevin Lin, on the other hand, used his social media far less often. His posts were much more reserved; often sharing not much more than economics articles written by various experts in his field. His profile picture was a shot of him in a business suit in Hyde Park, obviously posed. Despite the fact that they were twins, going by their social media they could not possibly have been more different.

Violet switched over to their Instagram accounts. Kevin Lin's was private, but Jenny Lin's wasn't. Most of the pictures were the same as on her Facebook feed; Jenny Lin certainly lived a life of luxury and travel. It looked like she'd already been to Asia three times this year, and it was only May! I wondered how good her grades were; I certainly could have never taken multiple days off every month and kept up even a remotely decent GPA.

As Violet continued to look up our victims online, I felt my eyelids getting heavy. The adrenaline from the crime scene was wearing off, and I was still working on just a few hours of sleep. I struggled to keep my eyes open; I knew I needed to stay awake.

WHEN I WOKE up on Violet's couch, with a blanket on top of me, I realized I must have fallen asleep after all.

"Oh good, you are awake," I heard Violet say. I groaned and looked up to see her, still dressed, drinking a smoothie that was a shade of green that humans just weren't designed to drink. Knowing Violet, however, I knew whatever she had planned for us didn't involve a pit stop at McDonalds. That smoothie probably even had kale in it.

"I guess I fell asleep," I said. "Thanks for putting me on the couch. How did you even manage that?" I asked, looking at her frame. Violet had to weigh a hundred and fifteen pounds, at best. I had at least thirty pounds on her. She just shrugged.

"You're not that heavy."

I eyed her up and down before realizing the futility of my attempts at getting any information out of Violet that she didn't want to give.

"Now, you have to get up. We are going to see some of Kevin and Jenny's friends. First, we'll be meeting some of Jenny's friends in thirty minutes."

I groaned as I rolled off the couch and hoped against all hope that wherever we were going, there was a Starbucks.

Twenty-five minutes later Violet and I were sitting outside the London School of Economics library. We were on a long concrete bench that doubled as a car barrier, next to an adorable statue of a little baby elephant. I gazed up at the gorgeous brick building with its white windows that just screamed classy academics, when three girls came up to us.

"Are you Violet?" one of them asked. She had just a hint of a Chinese accent.

"I am," Violet answered. "And this is Cassie."

"I am Cee-Cee," the girl replied.

"Sue," the brunette next to her said, holding out a hand. Her eyes were red; it was obvious she had been crying recently.

"And I'm Laurenne," the last one told us, as Violet motioned for them all to sit on the bench next to us. I let the three girls sit near Violet, and I sat on the far end, on the other side of Cee-Cee.

"I am sorry about your friend, first of all," Violet said, and the three girls muttered thank you.

"It's just so out of the blue," Laurenne burst in. "When I heard this morning, I just couldn't believe it. Jenny wasn't the type to get herself murdered."

"So you think there is a type?" Violet asked.

"Well, yeah. I mean, she didn't do drugs. She wasn't the kind of girl to get into fights at a bar. She didn't have a creepy ex-boyfriend stalking her. She lived a totally normal life."

"There is nobody in Jenny's life that you can think of who may have wanted her dead?" Violet asked.

"That's the weird thing," Sue said. "There really isn't. There was nothing strange about Jenny at all recently. She was supposed to go to Taiwan a few days ago, but then cancelled the trip at the last minute, but she said that was because she was too busy studying for exams. I don't blame her, I would have cancelled that trip too."

"There is one thing," Cee-Cee interrupted. "I do not know what it means. It may be nothing. But I need to say it, because if it helps catch the person who did this to Jenny, I want you to know. A few days ago, I saw Jenny on the street. I went up to say hi to her, but didn't realize she was on the phone. She was not the type to use her phone much, she almost always texted. So I thought it was strange that she was phoning someone. And then, I heard a little bit of the conversation. She told the person on the other end that she knew what she was doing, that everything was going to work out in the end and that no one would ever know."

"Do you know what she was talking about?" Violet asked, but Cee-Cee shook her head.

"No. She sounded… upset. Upset, and a little bit angry. I just left, and she never knew I saw her. I kept it to myself, but then when I found out about what happened, I couldn't help but wonder…" Cee-Cee trailed off.

"Don't worry," I told her. "There's nothing you could have done to prevent this." I didn't know if she was feeling guilty or not, but I was pretty sure that if she was, Violet certainly wasn't going to assuage those feelings.

Sue gave me a grateful smile in return.

"So none of you know what Jenny might have been

talking about in that conversation?" The other two girls shook their heads at Violet's question.

"All right, thanks," Violet told them, and the three girls left.

"I wonder who Jenny was talking to," I mused, and Violet shrugged her shoulders.

"I am more interested in what she was talking about, personally. But we cannot know. Not yet, anyway. We do not have enough information about the girl. Her friends were sadly not as helpful as I would have hoped. But no matter; we can get our information from other sources. For example, if I am not mistaken, here comes Ken Chu, a friend of Kevin Lin's."

Ken was a friendly looking guy in his early twenties, the kind that you just knew had an easy smile, despite his sombre face today as he made his way up to Violet.

"You're the woman investigating Kevin's death?"

"I am," she replied.

"Good. The more people that try and find who murdered his sister, the better. I'm not sure how I can help you though; I barely knew Jenny at all. Really just to say hi."

"Ah, but you misunderstand. Kevin was an intended victim in the blast," Violet told him. Kevin's eyebrows rose slightly.

"Kevin was murdered as well? I thought it was just bad luck that he came home when he did."

"The police likely think that. But the police are

idiots. I strongly believe the person who blew up that house knew that Kevin was going to be coming home, and that they set off the gas expecting him to turn on the light as soon as he entered the house."

"No way," Ken muttered, almost to himself, chewing on his lower lip. "I can't believe anyone would murder Kevin."

"Ah, but you have your suspicions about something," Violet said, her eyes beginning to gleam as she leaned forward. "It is obvious."

Ken shrugged. "I don't know. Maybe. I don't have anything solid, anyway."

"What do you think? Tell me everything; you never know what could be important later on."

"Well, it's just that for the last few weeks, Kevin's been a lot more stressed out than usual. He's been a little bit more distant, too. Forgetting about plans we've made, skipping classes, that sort of thing. He never used to do that before, it's totally out of the ordinary for him."

"Do you have your suspicions as to why?"

"Honestly, I thought he might have got himself a girl. Maybe someone his parents wouldn't approve of, hence the extra stress. I'm not sure, really. With exams and stuff, I was kind of caught up in my own stuff right now, you know?"

"Yes, of course," Violet said. "How close was Kevin with his sister?"

"They weren't extremely close," Ken replied. "Not

the kind to tell each other everything. But they shared that house on Bourne Road. It wasn't like they fought or anything like that, they just kind of lived like housemates. They each had their own lives, but they got along well enough all the same."

"All right, thank you," Violet told him, and Ken shook her hand.

"Please find the person who did this," he implored. "Kevin was a good guy. If someone killed him on purpose... I just can't believe someone out there could do that to a guy like Kev."

Violet watched Ken Chu's retreating back as he walked back in the direction of the library entrance.

"Well, I think what we have learned from Ken tells us that my theory that they were both murdered is even more likely to be correct."

"Because he was acting weird? Maybe he just had a girlfriend, like Ken said."

"From the research I did last night, I can practically guarantee he did not. A person beginning to act in a stressed manner only weeks before they are killed? I am very inclined to believe that whatever Kevin Lin was stressed about, it led to his death."

My phone suddenly buzzed in my purse. I pulled it out and found a text from my friend, Brianne.

Just finished a day at the hospital and I am knackered. Meet for a drink?

"Do you have anything else planned for us today?" I asked Violet, and she shook her head.

"No. I want to see the medical examiner to see the body, but he will not have had the time to do the autopsy yet. I will come by later and we will go together, all right?"

"Uh, yeah, sure," I replied, my heart dropping as I texted Brianne to tell her I could meet her straight away. I didn't really want to go to the morgue—I knew with my luck, Jake would be there.

Jake was one of the pathologists who worked at the morgue. He also happened to be hot as hell. I met him when I helped Violet solve four murders just after I arrived in London, and one day we ended up going on a date. It was really nice, he was amazing, but I hadn't seen him since.

Now enough time had passed that I was sure it was going to be awkward. I had always been the studious, nerdy type. I wasn't very good at dealing with members of the opposite sex. So, my totally rational plan had been to never go near the morgue again, and hope that I never came across Jake again, because then there wouldn't be any awkwardness. I knew that my plan was ridiculous, but I still didn't want to go see him later today.

"Ok, text me when you want to go," I told Violet. Maybe I could pretend to be violently ill, or something like that. For now, I was going to drown my woes in a beer with my one friend in England who was halfway normal.

CHAPTER 4

Brianne was short, with red hair, an infectious smile and a strong Australian accent. She was working her way through medical school here in London by working part time at Chipotle, which is where we'd met. As soon as I walked into The White Hart, which was mere steps away from the Royal London Hospital where Brianne did most of her studies these days, I saw her waving to me from a table in the corner.

I made my way through the slightly modern English pub interior, with its white walls and wooden accents, along the dark hardwood floor, past a mishmash of mismatched chairs and tables and the light brown bar, where the bartender was busy pouring ales to a group of doctors who had evidently come here to relax after their shift as well.

The smell of a traditional English roast wafted

through the place as I gave Brianne a quick hug and slipped into the rigid-backed—yet still oddly comfortable—chair across from her, resting my arms on the dark wood table.

"I'm so glad you came," Brianne said. "I could totally use a drink after today, and I always feel like such a loser when I sit here on my own."

"You could always go and hang out with them," I said, motioning to the crowd of male doctors who were getting rowdier and rowdier. Evidently they were a few drinks ahead of us. Brianne scrunched up her face.

"That's the kind of people I'm trying to avoid by inviting you here," she said.

"Oh, so really you didn't want to hang out with your friend, you just wanted a warm body to sit across from you and ward off the jocks," I teased, and Brianne stuck her tongue out at me.

"You also have to listen to me complain about my day," she replied, and I laughed as a waitress came by and handed us a couple menus with a smile.

"I'm going straight for the vodka orange double," Brianne said as she perused the menu.

"You have had a rough day," I said when the waitress left. "Going for the double straight away."

"And I'm going to down it before I eat any food so I can forget everything that happened today," Brianne added, leaning her head back. "What do you want to eat, I'll go up to the bar and order."

I told Brianne I wanted a Camden Hells beer and some fish and chips, and she got up, ignoring the catcalls from the doctors as she made her way to the bar.

"Man, I remember those days," I told her when she finally got back, thinking of my own days as a resident when I felt exactly the same way. "The feeling that everything is crazy and nothing is normal and everything is on fire. Tell me the war stories, I need to know."

"So first, just after nine last night, we get this guy in his twenties brought into accident and emergency. I don't even know what he was on, but it was some crazy stuff. First he tried ripping his IV out, screaming that we were from the Men in Black and trying to erase his memory. So it took four of us to hold him down and convince him that no, we were not in fact going to erase his memory. We sedated him, and that was the end of that, but man. Hallucinogens are getting weird these days."

"Oh, man," I said, shaking my head.

"That's not even top three on the worst parts of last night's shift though. About half an hour later, a woman came in with her husband. And she was big. Like, twenty-six stone big."

"How heavy is that in normal people numbers?" I asked.

"Uhhh... three hundred and fifty pounds or so? Maybe a bit more? You Americans, you totally don't get to make fun of the rest of the world for using weird and out-dated measurements," Brianne teased. "Anyway, so she comes in complaining of abdominal pain. The first thing I notice is there's this completely awful smell emanating from her."

"Uh oh."

"Yeah, exactly. So I start to move my hands under her panniculus, looking for any abnormalities." A panniculus was the fancy doctor term for a large fat roll. "I'm pressing around, trying to find the source of her pain, when suddenly I feel something weird. I grab it, and pull it out. It was a piece of fried chicken. At least, that's what I assume it was. It was covered in mould, and smelled worse than anything I've ever smelled before."

"Ahhhhhhh, that's so gross," I squealed, laughing.

"I know! So I threw out the chicken in one of the medical waste bins, because I was pretty sure it could walk on its own again, and it turned out she had gallstones and is having her gallbladder removed, but ugh."

Just then the waitress came by with our drinks and took our orders. While perusing the menu I realized that I hadn't eaten anything all day, and I was actually starving. I ordered the fish and chips while Brianne ordered a burger and fries—"after the shift I've had, I'm allowed all the calories I can eat today"—and she continued her tales from the shift from hell.

"And just when I thought that was all I could handle for the day, the coppers come along with a man. The man got a bit drunk and decided to rob a home. So he breaks into the place and is on the ground, rummaging through a box of video games. The homeowner wakes up and grabs his crossbow, sees the man on the ground and shoots him with it. Right in the anus."

I was laughing so hard I was almost crying. "Oh my God!"

"I know, right? So the cops are all around him, he's on his stomach on the gurney, crying out in pain, and has to go for emergency surgery. I swear, it's like the full moon came early this month."

It had long been a myth—that a large number of medical professionals believe in—that the full moon leads to more admissions and crazier happenings in the emergency room than at any other time of the month. Personally, I didn't believe in it. After all, that was crazy talk. But even those of us who didn't believe in it still referred to the "full moon effect".

"That sounds awful!"

"It was. Thankfully I didn't have to be involved with that surgery, because I got called in to watch over the next one, which was a guy who had a house blow up over him as he was walking home."

"Wait, in Belgravia?"

"Yeah, you heard about it?"

"I was there!" I quickly recounted everything about that night to Brianne. "So the guy is going to be ok?" I asked.

"Definitely. He suffered a bit of internal bleeding,

and he has a broken foot, and a broken clavicle, so he's not going to be comfortable for quite a while, but he'll survive. He's been coming in and out of consciousness; I only got to speak with him for a moment. I imagine in a few days he'll be starting to get back to normal."

"I'm really glad to hear that," I replied.

"Absolutely. I met his wife when he came out of surgery. She was beside herself with worry. They live on Cadogan Lane, apparently he was walking back from the tube to go home. She said he'd stayed at work late for the first time in ages, he was trying to get some sort of big deal worked out. He works for an insurance company in Holborn."

"Well all of a sudden I feel a lot less sorry for him," I joked.

"Hey, hey, hey. It's not like he's a lawyer or something," Brianne replied with a grin. "He was nice though. I stopped in on him, he wanted to know if anyone had died in the explosion, so I had to tell him about the two people living there."

"Ah, that sucks."

"Yeah. I guess it's better than having to tell family members about a death though."

"That's true."

The waitress brought our food by just then, and for the next few minutes Brianne and I ate in silence. The fish and chips were absolutely amazing. I had always been told that San Francisco had the best seafood in the world. And of course, that being American, we were the best at deep frying it. But I had to admit, as I bit into the crunchy haddock and followed it up with a perfectly crisp French fry and a forkful of mushy peas, the British absolutely had us beat when it came to fish and chips.

"So you're solving crimes with the crazy genius again?" Brianne asked, and I nodded.

"I guess so. I mean, how can you say no when someone calls you up at two in the morning and tells you to come look at a dead body's liver?"

Brianne laughed. "She's good for you though. She's absolutely insane, but she's good for you."

"Yeah, she is," I admitted. I had moved to London after a strong bout of depression, and I had to admit that I'd been spending a little bit too much time sitting in my flat, unable to muster up the energy to go outside for anything other than food and walking Biscuit before Violet's phone call.

"I'm totally going to want to meet her one day. I read an article on one of those online news sites the other week about her. Did you know she actually foiled a major terrorist plot in England last year?"

My eyebrows rose. "Did she really?"

"Yeah. The article was titled *England's greatest detective is actually French*."

I laughed. "If she sees it she'll be mad," I said, then put on a fake French accent. "Bah! I am the greatest detective not only in England, but the whole world! They could at least give me the proper credit!"

Brianne burst into a fit of giggles at my impression of Violet. "Is she really like that?"

"Yeah, she has an arrogant streak that she says she's earned. But if you look past that, she's genuinely a pretty nice person. She's just a bit... weird."

"I guess most geniuses are."

Suddenly my phone buzzed. Violet told me we were going to meet Jake at four that afternoon, three hours from now. I groaned.

"What?"

"Violet wants me to go to the morgue with her."

"So?"

"So Jake is totally going to be there."

"Yeah, and speaking of people who are weird... you're going to go, and you're going to have a normal adult conversation with him, because you are an adult, not a five year old. Stop hiding from the guy you like because you're being a weirdo."

I groaned. "I'm not being a weirdo about this. It's been so long now, it's *awkward*."

"It's only awkward if you make it awkward. Life happens. Besides, he knows you're messed up, because you admitted it to him on your first date. And you know he's a keeper because he didn't run away from you screaming right then and there."

I sunk my head onto the table. "I'm not good with dating. Why are you on his side, anyway? You're supposed to be *my* friend."

"I am your friend, that's why I'm giving you this

advice. Because I want you to bump naughty bits with the hot guy."

"Is that a medical term? Bumping naughty bits? Is that what they're teaching you in medical school?"

"Stop trying to distract me from my excellent love life advice," Brianne told me, wagging a finger at me. "It's not going to work. Go to the morgue. Act like a normal human being in front of Jake. Maybe he'll ask you out again. Maybe he won't. No matter what happens though, don't panic and ask him to marry you."

"I'm not *that* bad," I muttered.

"Just making sure," Brianne laughed.

"Fine," I sighed, exasperated. "I'll go, and I'll try not to look like an idiot."

"That's pretty much my goal every time I get out of bed in the morning," Brianne replied as she took a big swig of her drink.

CHAPTER 5

We finished eating and drinking around two, with Brianne begging off because she was sure she was about to nod off right there in the booth if she didn't get home soon. I headed back to my flat, certain that Biscuit was going to give me hell about not feeding him breakfast this morning. I figured I would feed the little guy—and maybe throw in a Temptations treat or two to beg for forgiveness—and then take him for a quick walk before heading over to the morgue.

Walking down Eldon Road, however, I quickly noticed something was wrong. And it wasn't that my detective powers were getting better, it was that six big, black SUVs were parked in front of Violet's townhouse. At first, I told myself it was none of my business. After all, Violet led a weird life. Maybe she was expecting visitors. Visitors who came in giant SUVs that I very rarely saw on the streets of London. This was a city of luxury sedans, fuel efficient Smart cars and scooters. I could count on one hand the number of times I'd seen an Escalade in this city, let alone six of them.

I went into my flat, where Biscuit immediately began meowing loudly at me. Evidently I was being scolded for forgetting breakfast.

"I know, I know, I'm sorry," I told him, putting some food in a bowl that he pounced on as soon as it hit the ground. As I listened to my little cat eating, I looked out my front window to Violet's place.

"Listen little guy, I'll be back soon, ok? At least, I hope so," I muttered as I went back out the door. I walked over to Violet's house, a gorgeous white building. Climbing the five or so steps to the front door, I put my hand up to knock, then realized that if Violet was truly in trouble, that wouldn't exactly be the smartest idea.

Instead, I slowly tried the door and found it was unlocked. As it creaked open, my breath caught in my throat. What if something really bad was happening? What if Violet was being held at gunpoint by a crazy person she'd had arrested in the past? I paused in the doorway as I heard voices coming from further back in the house. Wasn't the kitchen back there?

I gathered my nerves and forced myself to make my way through the study and back to the kitchen. I saw four men at first, they were all standing with their feet spread apart, hands in front of them. All of them wore dark suits. I didn't see any weapons. That was a good sign, at least.

As I walked down the study toward the kitchen, I stopped next to a wrought-iron floor lamp, grabbing it by one hand I called out "Violet, are you all right?"

Instantly the voices all stopped.

"I am fine, Cassie. You can come into the kitchen, it is all right. I am simply having a bit of a chat with some gentlemen from the government."

I tentatively let go of the lamp and made my way into the kitchen. Violet was sitting on top of the kitchen table, her legs crossed, an amused smile on her face. The men, on the other hand, looked like they'd just come from a funeral. Not a single one of them was smiling. There were four men against the wall, and one standing a few steps further forward.

"This is the woman you were with at the crime scene this morning," the man said.

"Congratulations, your observational powers are second to none," Violet replied, clapping her hands sarcastically. "I can see why MI5 has chosen you to lead this investigation." The man glared at her while I looked at Violet, confused.

"MI5?" I asked.

"Yes," the man replied. "I am Agent Tompkins from MI5. I am here to tell Miss Despuis here that she is no longer welcome to investigate the deaths of Jenny and Kevin Lin."

"The government says I am not allowed to do a lot of things," Violet said from her spot on the kitchen table. "I am not allowed to murder people. I am not allowed to vote in this country. I am not allowed to enter the City of London in a vehicle without paying a tax. And yet today I am honored by them sending me my very own secret agent to tell me that I am not allowed to do my job."

Agent Tompkins was obviously getting annoyed at Violet's glib demeanour, and I had to admit, I found it a little bit funny. A single vein in his neck began to pulsate as he took a deep breath before answering her.

"Your job is not to investigate murders. And while the police occasionally tolerate you because you solve cases for them, I do not tolerate it. You are not to investigate this murder."

"Ah, because you think you can solve it yourself, do you?"

"Yes, as we have done with thousands of other cases in the past, without your help."

"Oh I am not certain that is completely true," Violet said dreamily, her eyes moving to the ceiling. "In fact, I believe it was less than a year ago. But ah, I cannot speak of it. It is classified, and above your pay grade. But I can tell you that I most definitely have helped your organization in the past."

Two of the men against the wall dared share a

glance with each other while Agent Tompkins clenched his fists against his sides. Violet was definitely getting to him.

"I don't care what stories you're making up. This murder investigation has national security implications. The Prime Minister herself has made evident her desire to have this case cleared up as quickly as possible. I will not have an amateur running around playing Hercule Poirot."

"Ah, but I am not Hercule Poirot," Violet said, straightening herself up. "I am French, not Belgian."

"I don't give a sh…" Tompkins started before stopping and taking a breath. "I do not care what you think of yourself. I do not care where you are from. Stay the hell away from this murder investigation. You and your American friend. I'm warning you."

"I'm actually Canadian," I interrupted. I didn't know why I said it. I just thought it would be funny. Evidently, Violet did as well, though her smile was almost imperceptible.

"Yes, I can see the Queen's finest is on the case," Violet said, jumping off from the table.

"I don't care where she's from," Tompkins spat.

"Well, before you leave, I will give you a little bit of help," Violet said. "Kevin and Jenny Lin's father is Taiwanese. That is an island, off the coast of mainland China. I recommend you download Google Maps onto your phone and have a look before you visit the embassy. It would truly be embarrassing if you caused an international incident by visiting the embassy of the People's Republic of China instead. That one is the very big country in the middle of Asia."

This time I let out an audible giggle. Tompkins' face was starting to look strongly like a tomato.

"We're not done here," he growled as Violet headed back to the front door.

"Oh, but we are," she sang. "You've said your piece. You have come here thinking that I would be scared of parked cars and men in suits, waving your government credentials around in a way that makes me think you must be overcompensating for something. You do not want me to investigate a murder. I have understood. I simply disagree with your opinion that I am not needed. Also, I recommend that you take flowers to your wife tonight. She has not been pleased with you lately."

Violet stood in front of the door and waited patiently. Sure enough, a minute later, Tompkins made his way back to the door, his men following noiselessly behind. I could tell Tompkins wanted to ask about the comment about his wife, but kept his feelings to himself.

"As glib as you may be about the situation, I assure you, Miss Despuis, it is deathly serious," Tompkins said to her between clenched teeth as he stood on her doorstep. "If I find you messing around with this investigation, I will have you arrested and imprisoned."

Rather than answering, Violet simply closed the door in Tompkins' face.

Violet turned to me and broke into a giant grin. "Well, that certainly was an interesting conversation, was it not?"

"They were MI5. Why are the secret agents taking over this case?" I asked.

"Well, really MI5 is the equivalent of your FBI, or it is as close an approximation as is possible between the two agencies. I am not very surprised that MI5 has taken control of this case, although I did expect it to take at least twenty-four hours before they sunk their teeth into it. Because the victims were the children of a very high-level diplomat, MI5 is involved to make it seem as though the Crown sees this as being a case involving national security."

"But they were just college kids."

"College kids who possibly had access to important secrets. I remind you that as of yet we do not know what reason is behind their killings. Yes, if I was MI5 I would have taken over this case as well. Although, I likely would have put a slightly less pompous moron than Alexander Tompkins in charge of it."

"I gathered that the two of you didn't exactly get along. I saw a bunch of black SUVs in front of your place and thought maybe you were in trouble; that was why I came in."

If I wasn't mistaken, I thought I saw Violet's eyes soften slightly.

"Ah. Well I thank you, although I promise you, I had everything under control," she said, motioning for me to follow her to the front window. Violet drew away the blinds and waved down the street toward my house. I saw the figure of Mrs. Michaels, the eighty-something year old widow who served as my landlady. She was standing in front of her living room window, holding something against her hip... oh my God!

"Is that an Uzi?" I asked Violet incredulously as Mrs. Michaels casually returned the wave, as if they were just ordinary neighbors saying hello.

"Yes, you have good knowledge of guns," Violet complimented. At least, I thought it was a compliment.

"Well, I am American," I muttered. "Why does she have an Uzi? Isn't that illegal here?"

"Oh yes, but trust me, if the police ever raided that woman's home they would never find it. And there are a number of things in that home that are far more illegal than a simple machine gun."

My mouth was running dry. My new life in London was insane. "Why does she have an Uzi?"

"Mrs. Michaels is very protective of me. She would have noticed the SUVs as well, and been on the alert."

"So your bodyguard is an eighty-year-old widow?"

"Yes."

"Well that makes me feel safe," I deadpanned, and Violet turned to look at me.

"You make the mistake of underestimating her due to her age. I promise you, if there was a single person in this whole country that I wanted to watch over my property, it is Mrs. Michaels."

"That gun must certainly help," I said as Violet drew the blinds closed. "So I guess now our meeting at the morgue is off?" I couldn't deny that despite Brianne telling me I had to be an adult about this, I was a bit glad we were being forced off the case.

"No, of course not. Why would it be off?"

"Well, the guy from the intelligence service just told you you're no longer allowed to investigate this murder or he'll throw you in jail."

Violet waved off the threat. "Ah, do not worry. That does not mean that we must stop investigating. It simply means we must begin investigating more secretly."

Of course being threatened with prison was a threat Violet would just completely ignore.

"What was the comment at the end there, about his wife?"

Violet smiled slightly. "She is not happy with him, Tompkins' wife. His shirt has not been pressed, and she did not care to let him know before he left in the morning that he had a small bit of dried shaving cream behind his ear. However, she did see him before he left; there is a tiny bit of lipstick on his face, but it is on his cheek. She is not happy enough to kiss him on the mouth. He would do well to listen to my advice. Now, we go to see the good *docteur*?"

I sighed as I got ready to head down to the Coroner's Court in Westminster. It wasn't enough that we were hunting a murderer. Now we were hunting a murderer *and* had to stay away from the authorities while doing it.

And worse than all of that, I no longer had any more excuses to avoid Jake.

CHAPTER 6

Twenty minutes later Violet and I were standing in front of the quintessentially British looking, red-brick building that housed the Coroner's Court. Violet was in a bad mood; she had told me that since MI5 had taken over the case sooner than expected, the bodies would be gone, but she still wanted to pump Jake for any information he might have gotten before having the bodies requisitioned and taken back to MI5.

"Do you know if Jake is going to be in there?" I asked quietly as we stood outside the front doors of the building.

"I do not know. I assume so, as he is the best pathologist here. They would likely have made him come into work to look at these bodies."

I paused before the door when Violet answered. I

could see her wanting to roll her eyes, but to her credit, she simply stopped and put her hands on her hips.

"Why are you so afraid of seeing him?"

"I'm not afraid!" I protested.

"Then why are you standing in front of the door, refusing to move, like a frightened puppy?"

I had to admit, I had no good answer to that.

"I'm not, I'm just, uh, taking a minute to admire the building," I finally said. The lie sounded lame even to me.

"Well then, you continue to stare at bricks, I will go inside and help solve a murder."

Cursing silently to myself, I followed Violet as we entered the building and made our way to the elevators to take us down to the basement level that housed the morgue. We stepped out of the elevator and onto the clinical grey tiled floor. A minute later, Jake popped out of one of the offices along the side.

I couldn't deny that my stomach began to flutter with butterflies as soon as I set eyes on Jake Edmonds. A little bit over six feet tall, with tousled blonde hair and a broad chest, Jake looked like he belonged on the cover of a magazine, or maybe on a beach in Australia, holding a surfboard, rather than hunkered down in a morgue, cutting up bodies. When he smiled, dimples formed in his cheeks, and I swallowed hard, smiling at him, not trusting myself to talk.

"Miss Despuis," he said to Violet, nodding. "And

Cassie," he said, his smile growing into a grin. "I haven't seen you in ages," he said.

"Y-yeah… sorry," I stammered. "I've uhhh… been busy."

"Of course, yeah. I assume you're here looking for the Lin bodies?"

"I know, they are gone, are they not?" Violet sighed, and Jake nodded.

"Sorry, yeah. How do you know though?"

"MI5 paid her a visit, threatening to throw her in jail if she didn't stop investigating the murder."

Jake burst out laughing. "I bet she took that well."

"Well, we're here now, aren't we?" I replied, rolling my eyes slightly.

"If the two of you are finished," Violet said, "I have some questions about the bodies. I am hoping that Doctor Edmonds can answer them all the same."

"Yes, of course," Jake said, giving me a wink as he grabbed a file off a stainless steel counter. "I made a copy of everything I had when I heard MI5 were coming to pick up the bodies; I figured you would still come by."

"Thank you. It is always good when I work with people who are not complete *imbéciles*," Violet said, taking the file from Jake and flipping through it.

"The police at the scene noted your suspicion that Jenny Lin had been killed prior to the blast. It is one hundred percent correct. I can't tell you for sure what poison was used to poison her—"

"Arsenic," Violet interrupted.

"But it was most likely arsenic, as you say," Jake finished. "I did a biopsy of the liver and was ready to send it to the lab for a tox screen, but MI5 took it before I was able to send it away, so unfortunately I have no way of testing to be one hundred percent certain, but I am as certain as it's possible to be without scientific confirmation. There was also vomiting residue around the collar of the victim's shirt, implying that she had vomited not long before her death."

"And Kevin Lin?"

"It appears that he died in the blast. His organs were ruptured, there were signs of significant, high pressure trauma and he suffered from serious burns all over his body, but there were no other indications of anything else that might have caused his death."

Violet began to pace around the room. "So there is nothing at all that you can tell me that is new?"

"I didn't say that," Jake told her. "I just wanted to get the basics out of the way. Actually, I do have one thing that's a bit strange."

"Oh yes?" Violet asked, perking up.

"I must warn you, it is most likely nothing. In fact, the sample was so small, I briefly began to wonder if it was anything at all."

"What is it?" Violet asked, her eyes gleaming.

"Jenny Lin's hands were pretty well protected since she was curled up when the explosion happened, so I scraped under her fingernails. There wasn't much there, but under one of her pinkies was a trace of something. The flame test showed it was lead-based, then my other tests showed it was a carbonate. It was white lead. I have no idea how Jenny Lin could have possibly got trace amounts of white lead under her fingernails. From the way she was dressed and what I know about her, she didn't strike me as the type to be spending a lot of time in a mechanic's workshop in Taiwan, as the product has been banned in the UK for quite some time now."

"Ahhhh, but you do not have the creative mind!" Violet exclaimed.

"Hey, I just gave you something good, there's no need to insult me," Jake replied.

"But it is not an insult! You are the scientist. Everything must be reasonable and logical. But this! This changes things! I believe I now know why Jenny Lin was killed. Did you tell MI5 about the white lead?"

"I did, but that Agent Tompkins didn't seem very interested."

"He would not, of course. That is because he is an *imbécile* of the highest order. But the lead carbonate, that will be the key to solving this crime. I am certain of that!"

Violet began to pace around the room even faster now. I could practically hear her brain working at top speed. I looked over at Jake, who locked eyes with me and grinned.

"Always an adventure with Violet, right?" he asked me.

"You have no idea. Did I tell you she woke me up at two o'clock this morning to come look at Jenny Lin's liver and confirm the poisoning for her?"

Jake laughed, and the sound made me feel more comfortable around him. He wasn't acting like there was anything wrong. Maybe Brianne was right. Maybe I was the weird one.

"Hey, do you want to grab a coffee or something when you get some time?" Jake said. "Maybe after all this is over," he continued, motioning at Violet, who was now furiously typing away on her phone.

"Yeah, that sounds good," I said with a small smile.

"Cassie! Cassie come, we are going," Violet suddenly ordered, without taking her eyes off her phone.

"Well, I think that's my cue," I said. "We'll get coffee. It's a date," I even managed to stammer out before practically running to the elevator. My face was beet red and I couldn't help but start scolding myself. After all, I'd just had a normal, adult conversation with a guy. Ok, so that guy was hot as hell and way out of my league, but still! There was no reason for me to run away as soon as I said the word "date". What was I, twelve years old?

But I still couldn't help the little flutter of happiness in my belly. After all, nothing bad had happened. I didn't embarrass myself in front of Jake—not too badly, anyway. He didn't hate me, he didn't ignore me, and best of all he actually asked me on another date!

I was so happy about that, I forgot to ask Violet about what the lead carbonate meant until we were almost home in the taxi. When I finally asked she told me she had to do some more research, and she would be in touch, but that there likely wouldn't be anything more to do until the morning.

I got home, knowing I had to walk Biscuit straight away or I'd probably collapse from exhaustion.

CHAPTER 7

As soon as I walked into the door and grabbed the harness, Biscuit was a ball of energy. Luckily, he had been well enough trained to stand still for the harness, and as soon as it was on and we were out the door he was straining on the end of it like an overly enthusiastic puppy.

I laughed as I let myself be pulled along. When I'd first gotten Biscuit I was incredibly self-conscious about walking him in public. I felt like a crazy person. After all, who walks a cat? But Biscuit loved his walks, and slowly but surely I began to get used to it.

We turned left onto Victoria Road and ten minutes later—we had to take a couple of breaks to chase some stray leaves blowing in the wind—we were at the entrance to Kensington Gardens.

That I lived so close to these incredible Royal gardens still seemed incredible to me; here in the center of London, amongst the millions of people who lived and worked here every day, was this enormous park. It was filled with a combination of tourists and locals, and since I took Biscuit here almost every day, I was beginning to get to know a few of them.

I waved at Ivana, a girl from Slovenia who worked as a nanny and liked to speak to me to practice her English, even though her English was already pretty much perfect. She hurriedly waved back before trying to keep the toddler she was watching from tripping over a tree root as he ran after a dog chasing a Frisbee.

I took Biscuit along the broad walk, which was, as the name implied, one of the larger paths though the park. Biscuit happily trotted around in the grass next to the path, stopping occasionally to climb up one of the many tall, leafy trees that lined the park.

Every time I brought Biscuit here people wanted to pet him; after all, dogs in the park were no novelty, but it was rare to see a cat on a leash. Biscuit, luckily, was one hundred percent a people cat. He loved the attention, and the more pets he got, the happier he was. He even squirmed along the ground on his back, inviting people to rub his belly. Sometimes I thought my cat was a dog in a feline body. Then other times he'd throw up a hairball into my shoe and I knew that he was one hundred percent cat.

I waited as a five-year-old girl carefully pet Biscuit on the head; she giggled happily when he meowed contentedly, then as I looked up I saw a woman a few years older than me who had a nice little Yorkshire Terrier named Kiki. Kiki and Biscuit got along pretty well, we assumed it was because they were the same size, so I made my way over toward the bench she was sitting on.

"Hey, Linda," I said to her as I sat down, and she greeted me with a warm smile.

"Hi, Cassie," she told me in her super posh English accent. Linda was an executive at an advertising agency, and she was always impeccably dressed. It also helped that she was about five foot nine and looked like a model.

"How are things going?" Linda asked me as Biscuit went up to Kiki and they began to sniff each other.

"Oh, all right," I replied. "Violet is getting me to help her with that bombing in Belgravia. Although I'm not sure how much I'm helping anymore, there doesn't seem to be much more medical advice I can give other than "yes, that is a dead person" and I'm pretty sure she can figure that part out on her own."

Linda laughed. "Well, you never know. One day your medical knowledge might end up being the whole key to solving one of her cases. And as long as you're enjoying the work, then that's the important thing."

"I do. I have to admit, I find that following Violet around and watching her work is the most fun I've had since I've moved to London. It sounds macabre to admit, though. How about you, what have you been up to?"

"I met a man," Linda told me, giving me a sly look.

"Oooh, tell me!" I asked, leaning forward for the gossip. I had known Linda was single, but she also didn't seem especially interested in men.

"The story is such a stereotype. He's a client of the accounting firm the floor below us at the office, and so we ended up taking the lift together a few times. Apparently he's being audited, so he's having to see his accountant more than usual. Anyway, he asked me out last week and we had a casual lunch yesterday."

"What's his name?"

"Aaron. He looks like Channing Tatum."

"Stop right there. I don't need to know anything else. He's perfect," I said, and while Linda laughed, I noticed it sounded a little bit hollow.

"Wait, something is wrong," I said. I could definitely tell, Linda was keeping something about this story from me.

"It's nothing. At least, I think it's nothing. I'm just being paranoid."

"What is it?"

"Well, that's the thing. I don't actually have any solid proof of anything. I think I'm probably just being paranoid, since I haven't actually had a boyfriend in ages and I'm so scared that something's going to go belly-up." I waited patiently for Linda to continue, which she did a minute later. "But the other day when we were having coffee, we were talking about our families. Obviously we're both single, and I believed him when he said he had never been married. But then I was telling him about my sister, and how close we were growing up. He told me he didn't have any siblings, and I don't know, I just got the feeling he was lying to me, you know? But who lies about that? There's no reason to. So I was thinking maybe I was paranoid, and now I'm rambling, and I know I sound like a crazy person."

"No, no, not at all," I lied. She did sound a little bit insane. But at the same time, I understood where she was coming from. "So you think he was lying to you about having siblings?"

"I'm really not sure anymore. The more I think about it, the more I've been convincing myself that perhaps I've just got a bit of an overactive imagination," Linda said slowly. "But it seems no matter how hard I try, I can't shake the feeling that he was lying to me. But the thing is, I don't understand why he would."

"But you're afraid that if he's lying to you this early on in the relationship, that it's not going to work out?" I tried. I didn't know Linda very well, but I knew she was one of those women who did everything at one hundred percent. She was so busy with her high-powered job; she wasn't going to waste time with any guy that didn't have the potential to be *the one*.

"Exactly," she nodded. "I do feel a bit foolish, complaining about something so trivial."

"No, no, not at all," I appeased. I could actually see where she was coming from. If he was lying to her about something so trivial, why wouldn't he lie about other, more important things in the future?

"So anyway, I'm excited about the new relationship, but I can't get that sinking feeling out of my gut either."

"Do you want me to ask Violet to look into the guy for you?" I asked. I imagined for her this would be a thirty second job.

"Oh, no no, definitely not," Linda replied. "Thank you, but no. It's just my personal life, being as much of a mess as always. I'll sort it out myself in the end, don't worry."

"Ok, for sure. What did you say his name was?" I asked on a whim.

"Aaron. Aaron Stone. I hope it's just me being insane. He really is a nice guy."

"I hope it's just you being insane too," I laughed. "I'm sure it'll be fine, though."

"Maybe. Or maybe I'm just destined to be alone forever." And with that hopeful comment, Linda got up. "Thanks for being a good shoulder to whine on. I'm seeing him again tonight and I'm just hoping I don't mess it up too badly."

"Good luck," I said as I watched Linda and Kiki walk back toward Kensington Palace. Frowning, I took out my phone while Biscuit sat at my feet watching his friend leave.

"You'll get to see him again soon, I'm sure," I told Biscuit as I opened up my Facebook app and typed in the name "Aaron Stone".

The third profile down was obviously the guy Linda was describing. He certainly did bear a certain resemblance to Channing Tatum. I quickly scrolled through his profile, but there was nothing there that would obviously tell me whether or not he had siblings.

I sighed as I put the phone down. I didn't know what I was doing at all. Why was I looking this guy up? This was totally Violet's territory.

And yet, I couldn't help myself. I wanted to know whether or not Linda was right and he was lying about having siblings. As I got up and continued to walk Biscuit, it slowly dawned on me why I was doing this: I wanted to try my hand at a very simple problem. I wanted to pretend to be Violet, and solve problems, all on my own.

I smiled to myself. I wasn't a detective. I had no idea what I was doing. But I could give it a shot, right? After all, what could I possibly have to lose?

CHAPTER 8

When I went to bed that night just a little after eight o'clock, I had never felt like more of an old lady in my life. My Stanford days of pulling all-nighters before exams were definitely over. I'd slept for about three hours the night before and I was completely wiped.

I slept straight through until seven thirty the next morning when I woke up to a text from Violet.

Meet me at the Natural History Museum. Nine fifteen, front entrance.

I groaned and forced myself out of bed. Biscuit stretched and curled himself up in the warm spot I'd just vacated, and promptly fell right back to sleep. I muttered about how unfair it was that Biscuit got to be warm and comfortable while dragging myself to the shower.

Ninety minutes later I was showered, dressed, had

left some food out for Biscuit and grabbed a breakfast burrito and a latte from a coffee shop on the way to the Natural History Museum, which, was where I found myself taking one of the last few bites of my burrito when I saw Violet coming up toward me. She wrinkled her face when she saw what I was eating.

"Do they not teach people in America about the necessity of fruits and vegetables in a diet?" she asked me as she eyed the burrito.

"There's hash browns in here and potatoes are a vegetable," I replied haughtily. Not all of us wanted to eat a kale smoothie for breakfast. "Besides, I put some ketchup on it before too, and that counts as tomato," I said as I finished off the burrito.

Violet just shook her head as we made our way through to the entrance of the Natural History Museum. As we entered through the doors and into the building, my breath was completely taken away. The entrance hall was enormous, with ceilings that were at least fifty feet high. Gorgeous Roman arches lined every wall, and a large skeleton of a Diplodocus dinosaur towered over everyone, guarding the stairs behind that led toward the exhibits.

"His name is Dippy," Violet said, motioning toward the dinosaur as we moved past him. We made our way up the large staircase, but rather than going through an exhibit, Violet led me through one of the side doors and into the back alleyways of the museum.

We carefully made our way through a maze of

narrow corridors and small rooms that housed a number of objects that weren't ready for display on the museum floor. Eventually we reached a small office that was so filled with rocks it almost looked as though we were in a cave. Shelves lined the room from floor to ceiling, each covered with rocks and minerals ranging in size from that of a piece of gravel to a geode the size of a beach ball.

In the middle of the room, the rocks being used as paperweights, was a desk behind which was a small man with wire-rimmed glasses who must have weighed ninety pounds soaking wet. At a glance he looked to be in his late forties, maybe early fifties, and he ran his hands through his thinning hair as he muttered to himself while reading a textbook so large that it would have given Gray's Anatomy a run for its money, size-wise.

"Hello, Edward," Violet greeted the man cheerily, and he jumped to his feet.

"Ah! Violet! How good to see you again. What are you here for? Oh, and you brought a friend! Can I make you a cup of tea?" he asked, shuffling his way to a corner where a kettle and teapot were perched precariously on a thin table.

"No, thank you, Edward. We're fine. I called and set up a meeting with you, remember?"

"Oh yes, oh yes. Of course. Something about... oh dash it all, I cannot for the life of me remember what it was about."

"Lead carbonate," Violet replied.

"Of course, of course. White lead."

Violet turned to me. "Edward here is the most knowledgeable man in England in the field of Renaissance and Dutch Golden Age paintings. He's also an eminent expert on mineralogy."

I looked dubiously at the man in front of me, who was now fumbling around his desk in an attempt to find his glasses, which Violet deftly grabbed off the top of one of the shelves and handed to him. This guy didn't look like he was much of an expert in anything.

"Ah, thank you, Violet. Yes, yes, where were we. Right. White lead. Now, sit down," he motioned, but there was nowhere for us to sit. Violet simply leaned against the wall, and I stayed where I was.

"How much do you know about white lead?" he asked.

"It's a pigment that used to be used in painting," Violet said. "It was very common in oil painting to make very luminous whites. It also happens to be incredibly toxic."

"Yes, correct. A fact that was known during most of the paint's use, but accepted as a necessity in order to get the whites truly correct. Nowadays, titanium white is used in the stead of white lead to create a strong white tint in oil paintings, in large part because white lead has become nigh on impossible to obtain legally. But for two millennia, white lead was the main pigment to create white paint, before zinc whites came into style, and were eventually replaced with titanium white."

"I have a murder victim who was found with white lead under her fingernails. Her lifestyle doesn't fit the type of person who might accidentally come into contact with white lead in any kind of legitimate fashion. I believe she was smuggling stolen or missing art pieces from Europe into Taiwan, but I need to be able to find out what pieces she might have been moving recently. Can you help me with that?"

"Ohhh but that is juicy gossip," Edward told Violet, his head bobbing up and down. "There has, of course, been an emergence of a large market for western classic paintings in Asia these past few years. It is very lucrative, for those able to move the goods across borders without arousing suspicion."

"Being the child of an ambassador from the UK certainly would do that," Violet agreed.

"Oh yes. That is an excellent cover indeed. Now, there are certainly a large number of such paintings that could have been moved over the years. We have the Nazis to thank for that; they lost so many incredible artworks that belonged to Jews in mainland Europe that are now nigh on impossible to trace. So much time has passed, and in so many cases, those poor families all died, so no one was left to tell us that the paintings had at one point belonged to them…"

Edward trailed off, shaking his head sadly as he pulled an iPad from his desk. He began to type on it at a glacial pace. "However," he continued, "you say you're looking for a painting that might have been moved recently. I read about a theft the other day that I guarantee you the thieves would want out of the country as quickly as possible." After what felt like an eternity, Edward tapped a link on his screen and a picture appeared. He held out the iPad to Violet, who took it, and we both looked at the image for a second.

"This is…" I said softly, my voice trailing off.

"Yes," Violet finished for me. "It is Vermeer's masterpiece, The Milkmaid."

Even for someone like me, who didn't have any special knowledge of art besides what I learned in a first year undergrad Art History class years ago, the painting was recognizable. It featured a plump woman in a yellow and blue dress, wearing a white head covering, pouring milk into an earthenware container on a table next to a window. The painting was so realistic; it almost could have passed for a photograph.

"Exactly. It was only reported stolen four nights ago. The painting was in transit between the Rijksmuseum in Amsterdam where it usually stays, and a small, private gallery in Liverpool where it was supposed to start a tour of Europe over the next three months," Edward told us. "The museums involved had not notified the media as of yet, for fear of the negative publicity. However, they will not be able to hold them off for much longer."

"And I assume the white in this painting is white lead?"

Edward nodded. "Yes, Vermeer was known to be a common user of the tint. He not only used it directly, but also frequently used it to lighten his other shades as well."

"So if Jenny Lin had lightly scraped the painting before her death, say by accident, she would have had trace amounts of white lead under her nails," Violet said, almost to herself.

"But then that means that chances are the painting's been blown to bits, doesn't it?" I said worriedly. "If Jenny Lin had it, wouldn't she most likely have kept it in her home?"

Violet shook her head. "No. That does make the most sense, but think about it. If she stole the painting, or if it was stolen and given to her to smuggle, and she was killed for the painting, don't you think the thief would have made sure she had stored the painting elsewhere before blowing up the house? No, I do not think the painting was in the house. But a stolen priceless Vermeer about to be smuggled out of the country is an excellent motive for murder."

"So let me get this straight," I said. "You think that someone stole the paintings, that they were then given to Jenny Lin to smuggle into Taiwan, but before she was able to smuggle them out of the country she was killed?"

"Yes, *exactement*," Violet replied.

"But why? Did someone else want to steal the painting off her? It hasn't been in the news yet. No one should know that the painting was even stolen."

Edward wagged a finger at me, and I somehow felt shamed, like I was in second grade again.

"Oh no no, friend of Violet," he told me. "Not at all. There are people who know these things. I, for one, knew of the theft. The underground world all know of the theft."

"Ok," I sighed, feeling completely overwhelmed by everything I'd just learned. "So all the people who might want to steal from the thieves know about the theft."

"Yes," Edward said, nodding profusely. "That is a certainty."

"So basically we now have a suspect list that includes a whole bunch of criminals," I said, putting my head in my hands. Violet laughed.

"It is not as bad as you say," she told me. "Besides, if the case were easy to solve, then there would be no challenge."

"There's a lot more challenge here than we originally thought," I told Violet. "First the only challenge was figuring out who killed Jenny Lin. Then it turned out her brother was also a target, so we have to figure out what part he played in this. Jenny, and maybe also her brother, was involved in painting smuggling, and possibly the theft of one of the most famous Dutch

Masters' paintings in the world. And then on top of that, MI5 is pressuring you not to continue this case."

Saying all those words out loud made me feel so overwhelmed I was starting to get dizzy. The explosion had happened less than thirty-six hours earlier and already this case was getting so complicated I was wondering if even Violet could solve it, but she simply shrugged.

"I have solved much more difficult cases than this," she told me. "Ask me one day about the case I worked in Morocco. Thanks to that one I am the owner of sixteen hectares of land outside of Marrakesh."

Of course Violet would think this case was just a piece of cake. It only involved international smuggling of stolen masterpieces.

I pinched my nose to ward off the headache I could feel coming on.

As we left Edward in his office full of rocks and minerals and exited the museum, I could tell Violet was deep in thought. Her head was down and she wasn't watching where she was going; at one point I had to stop her from pitching headfirst down a flight of stairs.

"If you're going to think without watching where you're going, you might as well sit down while doing it," I scolded her. "Let's get some lunch or something."

Violet stared at me without saying anything for a good thirty seconds, and I was about to let her know that she was being incredibly creepy, when she finally nodded.

"Yes. Lunch is a good idea." She strode off at a blistering pace and I struggled to follow after her—while I no longer had any pain in my knee, I still had a tiny bit of a limp—and five minutes later we were in another one of those hipster cafés that Violet seemed to be able to conjure up out of nowhere. I couldn't wait until unhealthy food was back in style again.

I ordered the least healthy sounding thing on the menu—vegan mac and cheese with quinoa—while Violet ordered a smoothie bowl with extra chia seeds. When the waiter left, having taken our orders, Violet began to tap her fingers along the edge of the table, staring at a spot past me on the wall.

"Do you want to talk about it?" I prodded, and Violet nodded.

"Yes. There is something strange about this case."

"You mean besides the fact that this simple murder has turned into an international smuggling case?"

"Yes, beside that. I believe that we have to assume Jenny and Kevin Lin were working together. After all, it stands to reason that the person who killed them planned on killing them both, which I still believe. So they were both involved in the smuggling."

"But they couldn't have been the only two people involved. I've seen Ocean's Eleven; there would have to be more people involved."

"Yes. The pop culture reference aside, I simply cannot see Jenny and Kevin Lin as being the only people involved in this. It is possible, of course, but the chances of two people so young being that experienced in the heist of major works of art is unlikely. I suspect the actual thief is significantly older. Not to mention, the twins had no way of knowing the inner workings of the art market."

"So you think they were just the middlemen?"

"Yes. I imagine their only role is to smuggle the paintings into Taiwan."

"So we have to find out who they were working with."

"Well that part is relatively easy. They were smuggling masterpieces into Taiwan. They were working with a gang of Triads."

"Great, that was just what this case needed. An actual gang to be involved."

"Did you actually think that every art thief is a respectable man who wears a suit like your George Clooney?" Violet shook her head. "No. In fact, as with everything else, the large organizations are often the ones who must be looked at."

Just then, our food arrived.

"For now, we eat," Violet said. "Then after, we go to see if we can find the people with whom Jenny and Kevin Lin were working."

All of a sudden I felt a total loss of appetite, and it had nothing to do with the vegan cheese sauce on the noodles I was about to eat.

CHAPTER 9

"How do you know where to go?" I asked Violet. "I can't imagine you just hold a sign out in the middle of the street reading 'Triads please say hi, looking for a murderer'."

Violet cracked a smile. "No, certainly nothing quite so... crude. When you have worked in my line of work for as long as I have, you begin to know people. They tell you things. I know exactly where we will go to find the Triads we are after."

We finished our food and headed down to London Chinatown. Depending on who you ask in London, Chinatown is considered to be either in Soho, or just next to it. We crossed under the Chinese gate on Gerrard Street, with red Chinese lanterns criss-crossing the road. Everywhere I looked there was a different Chinese restaurant, souvenir shop, bakery or other Chinese-themed store. A hawker on the street tried to sell tourists souvenirs from London, and the air smelt of roasted meat and spices. Coming from San Francisco, this Chinatown seemed a bit small, but it was no less impressive than the one back home.

Violet let me down the main street, and into an unassuming shop selling souvenirs and random other wares. It seemed like every useable inch of space was taken up with either lucky cat dolls, containers of tea, chopsticks and other things that I didn't even recognize. The shopkeeper, a short woman who had to be at least in her seventies, eyed us suspiciously as we walked past, but Violet ignored her and immediately made her way to the back of the shop.

She pulled back the beaded curtain that blocked the back room from view and I followed her past stacks of boxes piled from floor to ceiling labeled with Chinese characters. The further we got from the street, the more uncomfortable I got. What were we doing here? We moved past the boxes, Violet pushing one of them aside completely, revealing a hidden concrete-walled hallway. Water dripped from somewhere and streaks of mud lined the floor. This was totally the sort of place where people were murdered. *I hope they find our bodies, give my mom some closure,* I thought to myself as we walked down the hidden hall, turned a corner and found ourselves face to face with the largest Chinese man I'd ever seen in my life.

He was at least six feet four inches tall, and built like an absolute tank. His neck had to be the size of my waist, for sure. He stood in front of a wooden door, and with his legs spread apart they spanned almost the whole doorframe. His large arms were crossed in front of him, and he peered out at Violet and me from behind a long set of bangs that grazed his eyelashes.

I wanted to stop. Every instinct in my body told me not to go near this huge guy in the back area of a shady shop in Chinatown. Nothing about this was a good idea, and my brain knew that. But Violet, completely relaxed, walked straight up to the man and stopped in front of him.

"*Guǎng jiāo yǒu, wú shēn jiāo,*" she said to the man in what sounded to me like impeccably fluent Mandarin. Of course Violet would be fluent. Immediately, he stepped aside and opened the door. This was totally not how I expected my day to go when I woke up this morning. Gathering my courage, I walked past the man and followed Violet into the room.

My nostrils were immediately met with the smell of cigarette smoke, both stale and fresh. Fresh smoke rose up to the ceiling, making a haze not unlike the morning fog at the top of the room. I struggled not to cough. The doctor in me knew just how dangerous smoking was for your health; the ten or so men in the room were all going to have major health problems later in life, I just knew it.

The light in the room was dim, and as my eyes adjusted I had a look around. The ten men were all seated around a green velvet table covered in mah-jong tiles. The game looked to be about half over, and there were stacks of bills—I could see English bills, Euros and a currency I didn't recognize that was probably Chinese Yuan—scattered across the table. All ten pairs of eyes were on Violet and I as we entered, and I couldn't help but notice one man reaching for his hip, where I wondered if he didn't have a hidden pistol.

This suddenly felt like a very, very bad idea. Maybe I could just turn around and leave. I could wait outside on the street for Violet to finish whatever it was she was trying to do here. Just then, I heard the door close behind me with a loud bang, heard the door lock click, and I winced. Violet and I were trapped in here now.

I looked around the room once more for a friendly face and found none. Every single one of these men were hostile, and I was sure at least one of them was armed. Then, a man at the far side of the table stood up. He was about medium height, maybe five foot ten inches tall. His black hair was cropped short, and he looked to be in his late thirties, but with a very hard face.

"Excuse me," he said in slightly broken English, "but you are lost, I think," he said.

Suddenly, Violet reached into her purse. She pulled out a handgun and pointed it directly at the man. Oh my God. This was not good.

There were cries of surprise and bustling from the men around the table. All of a sudden, seven of the ten men had pulled out guns themselves.

"Oh, you do not want to do that," Violet told them as I tried to subtly walk back toward the far wall. I didn't know what I expected to do there, it wasn't as though being a few feet further from the bullets was going to do anything to save my life, but I just didn't know what else to do. "You all put your guns down," she ordered. *"Fàngxià qiāng."*

The men looked at the man who had stood up, and Violet pointed the gun at him, and then spoke. "You know who I am. You know I work with the police. They know I am here. What do you think happens when I disappear from a Triad illegal gambling game? What do you think happens to you? Get rid of the men. We need to talk."

For a minute no one moved. The man was obviously considering Violet's words. She held her gun steady, her head high, aiming right at his forehead. I had a feeling that if Violet shot, she wouldn't miss.

"Gǔn kāi!" the man suddenly cried out. *"Nǐ gěi wǒ gǔn!"*

This was it. This was the end of my life. I was going to die in the middle of a firefight in an illegal Chinese casino in London. So much for moving to London because it was the safe option. I felt myself trying to find something to grab against the wall I was leaning on. I wanted something to hold onto when the bullets ripped through my body. I just hoped it wouldn't hurt.

But then, instead of firing on us, the men all began to move. They muttered to each other as they put their guns away. Violet and the other man were both staring each other down, as though the other men weren't even here. Violet kept her gun pointed at the head Chinese guy while the others all filed out of the room, the door magically unlocking and opening for them as they went to leave. I didn't dare look at any of them as they walked past me; I was all too aware of the fact that seven of the nine men had just pointed guns at me.

I'd grown up in America, and yet I could honestly say no one had ever pointed a loaded gun at me until today. The door lock clicked behind them, and Violet did the last thing I expected of her. She put her gun down, and laughed.

"Violet, Violet," the man said, breaking into a smile and coming around the table with his arms open wide. "It is always lovely to see you."

"And of course you, Lin Wei," Violet replied. "How is the family? Li Min has just started school, has she not?"

"Ah, but alas. She is wanting to be called by her English name now, Eva. It breaks her mother's heart."

"They are like that, children. But do not worry. In time, she will come to appreciate her heritage. For now, she simply wants to be like all the other children. But come, let me introduce my friend. Cassie, this is Lin Wei, the head of the Bamboo Revolution Triads," Violet told me, and she couldn't hide her smile when she saw me, still pressed against the wall. I was sure the color in my face was absolutely non-existent. "Ah, Cassie, do not worry. Lin Wei is a friend of mine, we simply had to put on a show until we could be in here alone."

"That show looked pretty real to me," I finally managed to mutter as I peeled myself off the wall and shook Lin Wei's hand.

"Oh, the guns, they were real. But do not worry, they would not have shot me without Lin Wei's approval."

"Which I would never give, of course. How could I deny the world the gifts of Violet Despuis? It is nice to meet you, Cassie. Any friend of Violet is a friend of mine."

"Well, you may change your mind about that when you learn about what it is I have come to discuss," Violet told him. Lin Wei motioned to the chairs the men had been sitting at.

"Sit, sit. May I offer you a cigarette?" he asked us both. I thanked him and declined, but Violet accepted. He handed her a cigarette and Violet cupped the flame of the lighter as Lin Wei lit it for her.

"Now," he said, leaning back in his chair. "I suspect I know why you are here, but all the same, you are much better at guessing than I am. You will tell me why you are here, and I will confirm."

"Jenny and Kevin Lin," Violet said, taking a deep drag of the cigarette and blowing the smoke back out slowly. It was obviously not her first cigarette, but I had never seen her smoke before, or smelled stale tobacco on her.

Lin Wei nodded slowly. "Yes. Yes, it is as I suspected. You have figured out more than MI5," he said with a smile, showing his tobacco-stained teeth. He didn't look unlike a shark ready to pounce on his prey, and despite the fact that Violet and he were obviously friends, I didn't trust him completely. Probably because of the whole having guns aimed at my head thing.

"Well that much is obvious," Violet said. "So they have not been poking around yet?"

"No. One of my men told me they took the case off the Metropolitan Police, but that is all."

Violet nodded. "Your information is good. MI5 is in charge of this case. This was not a good thing to happen if they make the connection."

Lin Wei nodded. "I agree with you. I can tell you with total honesty that we were surprised and dismayed to learn of Jenny and Kevin's untimely deaths."

"So you were not responsible for it, but they were smuggling paintings for you into Taiwan? And they were already in possession of The Milkmaid?"

Lin Wei smiled. "Every time you come to see me, I am always amazed at just how much information you know. It is no use denying it. Yes, the two children were smuggling paintings. It was generally Jenny, as officials are even less likely to suspect and check a woman's belongings, but Kevin was important as well. He acted as her protector and bodyguard, if anyone tried to question Jenny he would stop them, as a brother is supposed to do. As a tandem, they worked perfectly. And yes, they were already in possession of The Milkmaid. They had taken possession of it that same day. Do you know where the painting is?"

Violet shrugged. "I was hoping you would know. I only learned of its theft a few hours ago."

Lin Wei frowned. "No. We do not have it. When I saw you come in, I hoped that you would have a lead, and that you would be able to take the painting. I fear that it may be lost forever in the explosion."

Violet shook her head. "No, I do not think that. I was at the scene of the bombing. Jenny was murdered before the explosion, and it was set up in such a manner that I am certain Kevin was an intended victim as well. I believe whoever killed them possibly took your painting."

"Well, that complicates things."

"Who else knew about the theft? Besides the Bamboo Revolution, and you had no reason to want them dead. There are the other people in the industry who knew of the heist, but who else? Were you working with anyone on the outside?"

"That is the thing, we were not. Nearly every part of the heist was Triad-organized, except for the thief himself. He was not Triad, but if he wanted the painting, if he wanted to rip us off, he could have simply taken off with it. We would have hunted him down and killed him, of course, but if it turns out that he has killed the Lin children we will kill him anyway. We had another contact who is not Triad, but I have worked with him for twenty years. He is beyond reproach."

"So you're telling me you have no idea who had any reason to kill the kids, apart from the other people in the art world who knew of the theft."

"Exactly."

"And you had a buyer for the painting back in China?"

Lin Wei looked shrewdly at Violet. "You know I should not be telling you. But yes, we had a buyer organized. The painting was to stay in London for three weeks, to allow for time for the painting to get in and out of the news."

"And how long had you been planning to steal The Milkmaid?"

"It was a very quick decision. We had been planning for only two months, and the Lin children were told about it four weeks ago."

That was just before Kevin Lin began acting strangely, according to his friend Ken.

"All right. Thank you, Lin Wei. As always, it is a pleasure."

"Ah, but not at all. It is my pleasure. Your visits are always enlightening. And before you go, I would like to make you an offer."

"Yes?" Violet asked, not looking surprised at all.

"If you would be able to return the painting, if as you say it has not been destroyed, we would be willing to pay a large sum. Larger if you bring us the thief and murderer, as well."

"You will have to be more specific," Violet told him. "Are you talking seven figures? Eight?"

"Ten million pounds for the painting, five more if you also give us the thief."

"I will consider your offer," Violet told him. "Either way, I will be in touch."

Lin Wei nodded, and Violet turned to go back toward the door. I didn't really know what to do so I shot Lin Wei a smile, and followed Violet. As soon as she came close to the door the lock unclicked, and opened once more. I had a quick look around before we left but didn't see any cameras. They must have been very well hidden; there was no other way for the man on the other side of the door to know we were coming out.

We walked past the Chinese version of Arnold Schwarzenegger, then made our way back into the shop. Violet got ready to leave, but her way was blocked by the old lady manning the counter. She handed her a plastic bag filled with goods from the store. Violet thanked her and looked outside the shop worriedly. Great, that was what we needed - more trouble.

CHAPTER 10

"What's going on?" I asked, peering outside to see what had been noticed.

"It appears that we have been followed," Violet said. "Just follow my lead. Whatever you do, do not mention meeting Lin Wei in there."

Well, at least that didn't sound super ominous about what was about to come. Violet and I left the shop and she broke into a smile as Agent Tompkins immediately came over, the vein in his neck already beginning to pulse dangerously. Two other men walked behind him, obviously there to intimidate us.

"I told you to stay out of this," he said, but Violet simply looked at him, surprised.

"Stay out of what? The murder case? We're just doing some shopping in Chinatown," she said, holding up the bag.

"Let me see that," Tompkins ordered, snatching the

bag from Violet's hands and combing through the contents. There were a few packs of tea and a small piece of ginger root in the bag. Frowning, Tompkins had no choice but to hand the bag back to Violet.

"This shop is owned by the UK leader of the second biggest group of Triads in Taiwan," he said through gritted teeth.

"Is it?" Violet asked, looking at me. I tried to look appropriately shocked. "I had no idea! After all, as you were so quick to point out yesterday, I am not a member of law enforcement, I am simply an ordinary member of the public. People like me do not know things like that. I simply came to refill my tea supply. After all, this is England, you do drink tea here."

I knew Violet was antagonizing Tompkins on purpose. They both knew that she had been there to visit Lin Wei, but he had no way to prove it.

"Besides," Violet continued. "You are welcome to go into the shop. It is manned by a little old lady. She must be barely four feet tall and eighty years old. I do not know what the leader of this Triad gang you mentioned looks like, but I honestly cannot see such a frail old woman being in charge of a major gang."

Tompkins nodded almost imperceptibly and one of the two men behind him went into the shop, while Violet watched Tompkins with a small smile on her face. The man came back out a minute later, shook his head quickly, and went back to stand next to the other man in black.

"So you see? I could not have been here to see whoever this man was."

"You were at the Museum of Natural History this morning as well," Tompkins said.

"I was."

"I want to know why."

"You would like to know why I went to visit one of the most impressive museums in the world?"

"That's what I said, don't play dumb."

"Oh believe me, I am not the one looking dumb in this conversation. Try to learn everything about something, and something about everything."

"What is that supposed to mean?"

"It is a quote by Thomas Huxley. There you are, now you have learned something about an English biologist. That is your 'something' for the day. I was at the museum to look at the exhibits with my friend, who is new to England. She had never been to the museum, so we decided to spend the morning there. Besides, what could I possibly have learned about the murder in a museum filled with dinosaur bones and images of constellations?"

Tompkins' face was fast approaching a shade that could only be described as fire truck red.

"I know you're lying. I'm watching you," Tompkins spat out at last. "I know you're working this case. If I find proof, I *will* have you arrested. You've been warned."

"You may want to spend your time finding the

murderer," Violet told him. "I may not be investigating, but I have my sources, and I have heard that you have yet to discover the motive for the crime. Let that be a hint to you," she added in a sing-song voice as she began walking back down the street.

"So now MI5 is watching you," I said. "Because this wasn't weird enough a day already."

"Yes, they are watching me. I should have suspected. I thought Tompkins would have been too busy actually trying to solve this case rather than following me, but it seems that much like a child who has not the knowledge to get good marks on his own, he has decided to cheat on the exam."

"He's following you to find out what you know?"

"Even Tompkins would not be so foolish as to follow me simply because he hates me," Violet replied. "In fact, I would not be surprised if his boss recommended this course of action. His boss was once made very familiar with the success rate of my methods."

"So what do you do now?"

"Now I simply have to be more careful. Especially as I would like to speak with the Ambassador himself. He has returned to the UK, obviously. We can no longer attend the funeral, but that is all right. We will gain audience with him all the same."

"And what if Tompkins sees us?"

"Then he will threaten to arrest us once more."

"That doesn't bother you?"

Violet shrugged. "It would not be the first time."

"I swear, one day you have to write a memoir," I muttered as we made our way down the street with the tea and ginger given to us by the lady running the shop fronting for the Triads.

* * *

Violet hailed us a cab, but during the twenty minute ride back to our apartment, she began to brood.

"What's wrong?" I asked her. "I thought you got a bunch of information from Lin Wei."

"I did," Violet said, "but some of it was wrong. And I don't think he was lying to me, so it means I am missing something."

"What's wrong about it?"

"The sum he offered me as a reward if I were to find the painting."

"Ten million pounds? What, were you expecting more?" I joked. Ten million pounds was about twelve million dollars. Not a bad commission for a detective. Violet shook her head though, completely serious.

"No. No, that is the problem. He has offered me *too much*."

"Wait, you're not going to take it, are you?"

"Of course not. If I find the painting I will give it back to the authorities. I may not be the most appreciative of the arts, but even I understand that a painting of that provenance belongs in a museum for all to see, not hidden on the wall of a corrupt businessman."

"So what's the problem?"

"How much do you know about art theft?"

"Well, on top of what Edward mentioned this morning," I started cheerfully, "absolutely nothing," I finished. "Ok, that's not entirely true. I know that the Mona Lisa was stolen back in the early 1900s and then they found it again a few years later. An Italian guy had taken it. That's really it though."

Violet nodded. "You know as much as the average amateur, then. The secret is that art is notoriously simple to steal."

"Really? They make it look so hard in the movies."

"The reality is that apart from a few major museums—and even then security can be very lacklustre—most major artworks are displayed in small galleries that do not nearly have the budget required to adequately secure a painting. And once a painting is stolen, it is actually quite rare for it to be recovered. Since we are talking about The Milkmaid, which is a Vermeer, there was a Vermeer stolen in 1990 worth around one hundred and fifty million pounds, called The Concert. It has never been recovered."

"Wow, that's incredible," I said, astounded.

"Yes. The painting, along with twelve others stolen on the same night, were taken from the Isabella Stewart Gardner museum in Boston. It is the perfect example of a museum of a personal collection which was plundered. In total the thieves managed to steal four hundred million pounds worth of art by dressing as policemen and breaking into the museum at night."

"And none of it was ever recovered?"

"No," Violet shook her head. "Your FBI continue to investigate."

"So it sounds like art theft is a pretty lucrative business, where's the problem?" I asked. "The Milkmaid would surely be worth one hundred million pounds, wouldn't it?"

Violet nodded. "Yes, it would. But the problem with art theft is that stolen goods are essentially worthless. Hot paintings are worth perhaps ten percent of their market value. In fact, the main value from a stolen painting is to essentially bribe the company that has insured it. Say you steal a painting worth and insured for fifty million pounds. You could sell it for maybe five million pounds, if you are lucky. However, you can go to the insurance company, and offer them the painting in exchange for ten million pounds. That way, they do not have to pay out the full fifty million."

"Seriously? That actually works?" I asked, incredulous. Violet nodded.

"Yes. But that is why something here does not make sense. Even if we assume that The Milkmaid is worth one hundred million pounds—keeping in mind that estimate may be very high, as the last Vermeer to sell at auction sold for sixteen million pounds—ten percent of the value is only ten million pounds. Which is what Lin Wei offered me in exchange for its recovery. He would never have offered me the full value of the painting to him, but his plan could not have been to bribe the insurance company either, as he was planning to smuggle it out of the country. And that is what is bothering me."

"What if he's simply found a buyer in China or Taiwan willing to pay more than the painting's value?" I asked, but Violet shook her head.

"No. The people in China who have the money to spend on stolen masterpieces are not the type of people who would allow themselves to be—how do you say—ripped off."

"So basically the Triads are hiding something, and you don't know what."

"*Exactement.* However, I do not think they are responsible for the deaths. Lin Wei is right, he had no reason to have them killed. They were an asset to him, and their deaths will likely interrupt his smuggling business until he finds a new, safe way to move stolen paintings."

"This case is so much more complicated than I expected," I complained as the taxi pulled up to the curb in front of Violet's house.

"I told you it would be interesting," she replied with a smile.

CHAPTER 11

Violet told me she needed some time to think about the case, and I made my way back into the apartment. After playing with Biscuit for about half an hour, I pulled up my iPad and decided to see how well I could play detective myself. I was going to find out for Linda whether or not she was right about Aaron Stone not having any siblings.

I decided that the first thing to do was what Violet always did: check out his social media accounts. I opened up Facebook and typed "Aaron Stone" into the search bar. Since I'd already done the search before, I knew what profile to look for. I got a better look at Aaron Stone's profile on my iPad than on my phone: he did look quite a bit like Channing Tatum. He had the same squinty eyes and pouty mouth, along with brown hair that was admittedly a little bit longer than Channing Tatum usually had it, but it was close enough.

I clicked on his profile, and to my dismay, almost everything was private.

"Of course this always works for Violet," I muttered to myself while Biscuit climbed up on my lap and began to purr. Apparently he was jealous of the iPad getting more attention than he was. I stroked him gently while looking at the few posts that were public. Aaron Stone had shared a post about how men could help with feminism by calling out their friends when they made misogynist comments in public. He had signed a petition calling for tougher penalties on people breaking the fox hunting ban in England. He had updated his profile and cover photo a few times; one showed him skiing in the Alps somewhere, another was a picture taken of a lake somewhere. While it seemed like he was a decent guy, none of this gave me any actual insight into his life or, more importantly, as to whether he had any siblings.

Luckily for me, however, I did notice that one of the pictures he had set to public he had uploaded from Instagram. I clicked the link and was taken to his Instagram page, which thankfully wasn't set to private. Maybe here I could glean a little bit more information.

Sadly, though, I wasn't able to find much about him. It seemed Aaron Stone was the type to post one picture every few months, with a few hashtags and not much more. It did seem that Aaron Stone was a fan of food—or more specifically, desserts. Almost every picture he posted was of a different batch of cookies he had made, or cakes he'd bought, or macaroons he'd been given as a gift. He also didn't garner a lot of likes or comments. There were one or two other men who commented on his photos regularly, but clicking on their profiles showed that they were obviously not related to Aaron. One of them, Anthony Myers, was black, and the other, Joseph Han, was born and raised in Korea, apparently. By the time I was finished scanning through his pictures I was none the wiser as to his family history, but my stomach was growling and craving something sweet.

As I looked out the window, however, I noticed that the clouds were rolling in and threatening to open up and unleash a torrent on London. Like a true San Francisco girl, I was *so* not used to walking in the rain like Londoners, so I decided I'd make do with whatever was in my kitchen.

Luckily, my passion for pancakes meant I had everything I needed to make chocolate chip cookies in the cupboards already, so I began making those, thinking about how good it was to feel like actually *making* something again.

After I had been hit by the car back in San Francisco, it turned out that my mental injuries took a lot longer to heal than the physical ones. While I still had a scar on my leg, and a slight limp most of the time, after the accident I fell into a deep depression. Moving to London was an attempt to change my environment and force myself to get over the fact that I was never going to be a surgeon, and get back into life.

It had worked with mixed results; when I had worked with Violet on her last case, I found myself with more energy, and actually going outside, which was a marked improvement on my life in San Francisco. However, when the case had ended, I quickly found myself turning back to old comforts, and occasionally being hit with the depressive stage of lying in bed, being completely unable to move.

Biscuit helped, of course. Having another mouth to feed forced me out of bed quite a few times when I otherwise would have stayed in, and having to walk him made me go outside. But one thing was certain: whenever I followed Violet around on one of her cases, I definitely felt a lot more active, and I almost felt like my old self again.

When I wasn't afraid for my life, anyway.

Mixing the ingredients together in the bowl was relaxing—trying to stop Biscuit from "helping" without touching his fur with my food-covered hands was less so—and forty minutes later I triumphantly looked at two dozen chocolate chip cookies. Biscuit hungrily eyed the six little chocolate-free cookies that I'd made for him as well; it wasn't the healthiest treat ever for a cat, but then again cookies weren't that healthy for humans either.

I sat in front of the TV and watched the end of a random current events show while I enjoyed a couple cookies, then I looked at the stacked plate and realized there was no way I was ever going to be able to eat that many cookies.

Well, maybe that wasn't entirely true. But there was no way I *should* eat that many cookies in just a couple of days. I didn't exercise enough these days to justify it, not even close. So instead, I piled most of the cookies on a plate and decided to head upstairs and offer them to Mrs. Michaels, my elderly landlady. After all, not only was it a nice thing to do, but going from the snatches of information I'd gotten from Violet, and the couple of conversations I'd had with the woman herself, Mrs. Michaels had led a very interesting life. I wasn't going to lie, I hoped that by bribing her with cookies I might get some details into that former life.

I gave Biscuit one of the special kitty cookies I'd set aside, grabbed the plate and made my way up the steps and knocked on Mrs. Michaels' door. A few seconds later she opened the door and greeted me with a huge smile.

"Ah! Cassie! My favorite tenant! Come inside, come inside, it's going to rain," she insisted as I stepped over the threshold and into her house. "Oh and you've brought biscuits! How lovely. Your generation does not cook enough, it is good to see a young woman like you who still knows how to use an oven."

I laughed. "Well don't go overboard, you haven't tasted them yet," I told her.

"Oh but I can smell them, and they don't smell like

rubbish," she told me, and I laughed as I took off my shoes. "I hope you don't mind that I have another visitor," she told me.

"I can come back, if that's more convenient," I said, suddenly feeling a bit awkward.

"Oh no no, not at all. Come on in," Mrs. Michaels insisted. Feeling slightly uncomfortable, I followed her to her living room, which was surprisingly modern for such an old woman. There wasn't a single piece of lace or gaudy printed sofa cover in sight. Instead, a long, light grey leather couch lined one of the white walls, decorated with colorful abstract paintings. On top of a bright blue rug on the ground was a black wooden coffee table, and a couple of grey armchairs to match the couch were on the other side. The whole scene looked like it could have come out of an interior design magazine.

Sitting on one side of the grey couch was Violet, happily sipping tea from a delicate china cup. If she was surprised to see me up here, she didn't act like it.

"Ah, Cassie," she said. "What a nice surprise!"

"What are you doing here?" I blurted out. Violet didn't seem to me to be the kind of person who would just drop by a neighbor's house for afternoon tea.

"I am trying to work through our little problem with the help of Mrs. Michaels," Violet told me.

"Our little problem? You mean the double murder?"

"I do." Of course Violet would refer to it as a "little problem". Mrs. Michaels bustled in with the cookies on a plate and an extra teacup, along with a pot of tea.

"Sit, sit," she implored as I settled onto the other end of the sofa from Violet. I thanked Mrs. Michaels as I took a cup of tea, and she offered Violet a cookie.

"I have seen the way Cassie eats, I am sure I would not approve of what is in this," Violet said, but I couldn't help but smile slightly when she took a cookie anyway.

"If there's one thing the Americans have truly mastered it's the biscuit," Mrs. Michaels said, taking a big, unladylike bite of her cookie. "Although biscuit is a much better name for them than cookie," she said.

"Well our biscuits are something completely different," I explained, but Mrs. Michaels nodded enthusiastically.

"Yes, yes, of course. That travesty that you call a biscuit is a complete butchering of our savory scones," she said with such fervor that I was almost afraid to disagree. I had already had a gun pointed at me this week, I didn't want to die at the hands of an old lady who was offended by American cooking. Luckily, Violet interrupted before I had a chance to reply.

"So Mrs. Michaels, I had just finished telling you what I'd learned," Violet started, but she was interrupted before she could continue. I wondered how long it had taken for Violet to get through her whole story when Mrs. Michaels' interruptions were factored in.

"Yes, yes, of course darling. That whole matter with the stolen painting. That was a good take, that one. Although personally, I was never one for paintings. It is simply too difficult to truly get good resale value. I would still recommend it to beginners attempting to get their feet wet, however."

My mouth dropped open at Mrs. Michaels. Was she seriously giving Violet advice about painting theft? There was so much more to this woman than I could have ever imagined.

"Yes, that is my problem," Violet said. "The resale value. The Chinese, they have offered me ten million pounds if I recover the painting. But it would not be worth more than one hundred, I imagine."

"Well then my dear, there are two scenarios," Mrs. Michaels said. "Either they've found a buyer willing to pay way more than the price for hot goods—"

Violet shook her head no. "No, I do not think that is happening."

"Then they have multiple buyers," Mrs. Michaels said conspiratorially.

"Of course!" Violet exclaimed, but I just looked at the two of them blankly.

"Multiple buyers?" I asked. Mrs. Michaels turned toward me.

"Yes," Mrs. Michaels nodded. "It's not done very often, because it requires extensive resources and, as you young ones say, balls of steel. I can think of at least one instance when a thief was caught and killed for it.

Of course, the reason behind the killing was never discovered, and the perpetrator never found. But it only works on paintings of extraordinary fame, such as The Milkmaid. Essentially, the thief has copies made of the stolen art. And when I say copies, I mean there are perhaps five people in all of England who could make copies of the quality required. Then, the thief sells the painting. If he can get ten million pounds for it, he sells five of them. Just like that, he has made fifty million pounds."

"And he advertises to all of the buyers that they're getting the real thing, and not a fake?"

"That's exactly it."

"So you think that the Triads are making multiple copies of the painting and selling them off to different investors as the original," I continued, the wheels turning in my head. "And the reason it has to be a famous painting is that it will make the news; so the thief can prove that the original painting was stolen. And also, someone who has a famous painting in their home would be less likely to brag about it than someone with a random painting from a no-name artist?" I ventured as a guess.

"Ah! She is a clever one, your new friend," Mrs. Michaels said to Violet. "Yes, that is the reason why."

"Well I certainly do not make a habit of making friends with idiots," Violet replied, taking another sip of tea.

"No, you don't, do you dear."

"Your explanation about the multiple fakes is the most reasonable solution I can think of," Violet said. "Of course, I am not surprised the Triads were playing a dangerous game."

"Why don't you report Lin Wei to the police?" I asked. "After all, you say he's the UK leader of one of the biggest gangs of Triads in Taiwan, wouldn't the cops here love to lock him up?"

Violet gave me a crooked smile. "I would love to. And Lin Wei knows it. However, we reach an impasse when it comes to proving his crimes. Lin Wei is extremely careful. He is never directly linked to any crimes whatsoever; he makes very sure of that. I have never been able to link him to a crime, and likely never will be able to. He knows it, which is why he is willing to talk to me. That, and thanks to me one of his biggest rivals is now spending the rest of his life in prison. He has been much friendlier toward me since I made that happen."

"So he knows that if you ever find proof linking him to a crime that you'll report him?" I asked.

"Oh yes. He is very well aware. But he knows that he can admit things to me that I will never be able to link back to him. And of course, in England, if I were to record the conversations between us, they would not be valid in court."

"What I'm most curious about is how the Triads found out the painting was going to be moved, and how they got the details," Mrs. Michaels chimed in.

"After all, it was being kept in a Dutch museum. I may be wrong, but I imagine the Triads have very little presence in the Netherlands. Certainly not enough to get a man deep enough to know the details of the move."

"Mrs. Michaels!" Violet exclaimed. "You are a genius of incredible proportions. I knew there was a reason I came to see you."

"Ah, so it wasn't simply for the tea and the excellent conversation?" Mrs. Michaels teased with a glimmer in her eye.

"There is always that," Violet replied with a smile as she reached for another one of my cookies.

"So why does Mrs. Michaels know so much about art theft, anyway?" I asked, and both women looked at each other.

"Well dearie, when you get to be my age, you eventually gain a lot of knowledge about a lot of things," Mrs. Michaels said to me, and it was one of the least convincing lies I'd ever heard.

"Oh come on," I laughed. "I've got a grandmother too, and I guarantee you she doesn't know anything about the details of stealing million dollar paintings."

"Ah, well, then I suppose I may as well tell you the truth. My husband, before he died, was a wee bit of a naughty boy. I learned these things from him; he was an expert."

"Ah," I replied, but I had a feeling Mrs. Michaels was still hiding things from me. I had never been so suspicious about people before moving to London, but it seemed that everyone Violet knew had some sort of interesting past.

Maybe Aaron Stone wasn't going to be the only person I'd be researching over the next few days.

CHAPTER 12

After having tea with Violet and Mrs. Michaels, Violet told me she had a bunch of research to do and that she would be in touch the next time she had anything substantial to share or for us to do. However, it turned out I didn't have that long to wait. That night around ten pm I got a text from Violet asking me to come over, and to just walk in instead of knocking.

I did as requested and quickly discovered why going to the door was going to be such a hardship for Violet. Her entire study floor was covered in papers, save for a tiny spot in the middle where she was seated, her legs crossed and leaning so far over the sheet of paper directly in front of her that it would have made any yoga teacher proud. Her face had to be about an inch from the letters.

"Violet?" I asked cautiously. She was so dead still it was almost unbelievable.

"Ah, Cassie. *Bien,* come here," she said. "Pay no mind to the papers," she continued, waving a hand, noticing my trepidation. I carefully made my way toward her, trying to disturb her work as little as possible all the same.

"What have you found?" I asked. "This must have taken hours to go through."

"I have not yet sorted through all of it, of course. There is too much for that, and I did not receive this pile until a couple of hours ago."

"What is it?" I asked.

"It is a number of credit card statements that had belonged to Jenny Lin. Someone rang my doorbell and left them. They were dropped on my doorstep and the bell rung, but the person who left them did not identify him or herself."

"Wait, so you're trying to tell me someone dropped all of Jenny Lin's credit card records on your doorstep and you have no idea who it was?"

"I did not say I had no idea who it was," Violet corrected, "I simply said they did not stay to identify themselves."

"Well who was it then?"

"When you watch your American TV shows about crime, in which the police are the good guys, what happens when the FBI takes over a case?"

"The cops always resent them for taking it," I answered.

"Well, it is the same in England. When MI5 took over this murder investigation, it would have ruffled quite a large number of feathers at the Metropolitan Police. Not only would they have wanted to keep the case themselves for reasons of pride, but also they would feel that MI5 have only involved themselves to get the glory when they finally solve the case."

"So you think someone from the police left the box of files here for you to find so that you'll solve the case before Tompkins does," I finished, nodding slowly. "But I thought everyone at the police hated you."

"It is only *most* people at the police who hate me," Violet corrected, and I smiled at how easily she admitted it. "However, everyone at the police hate MI5, and even those that hate me, hate them more."

"So this is an 'enemy of my enemy is my friend' kind of situation then," I said, shaking my head slightly.

"Yes, it is," Violet said.

"What did you find in Jenny's financial records?" I asked.

"A lot of spending at luxury stores in the city. Let us simply say that your large insurance settlement for your injury would not have funded Jenny Lin's lifestyle for very long."

"Wow," I muttered. I'd received a payout of a little over ten million dollars in lost future earnings, pain and suffering, and all that sort of thing after my mom immediately contacted a lawyer when I was hit by that car. Up until now, apart from spending around one hundred grand to pay off all of my student loans, I had spent just over two thousand dollars of it, and that included my plane tickets to Europe. I'd had the money for just over three months now. In fact, I was fairly certain I'd already earned more than two grand in interest. I knew the money had to last me the rest of my life; I wasn't about to go around spending it willy-nilly.

"But," Violet continued, handing me the sheet she had been poring over, "I believe I have found something else as well. Fourth line down."

It was a credit card statement for a statement period that ended just five weeks earlier. The first few lines made the part of me that had been a starving student for so long cringe: Louis Vuitton—two thousand pounds. The Cuckoo club, one of London's most exclusive nightclubs—nine hundred and seventy pounds. Harrods—twelve hundred pounds. But then, as Violet said, there was something interesting on the fourth line.

Jenny Lin had spent sixty pounds every month to rent a self-storage locker in Mitcham.

UK's Best Self Storage—Mitcham, read the charge line.

"Where on earth is Mitcham?" I had to ask Violet. By now I had lived in London for long enough that I knew most of the major suburbs and neighborhoods around London, but I had never heard of this one.

"In the southwest, it's about a forty minute drive from here. She's kept that storage locker for at least the past year, as far as I can tell."

"Forty minutes," I muttered. "That's incredibly far. I've seen ads on the tube for self-storage places that are barely outside of Central London, and it's not like the money would be an object for someone who—I glanced at the rest of the statement—spent four hundred and seventy two pounds this month at Victoria's Secret."

"*Exactement*," Violet said excitedly. "Ah, Cassie, you are getting better at deducing! It is strange! Why would someone like Jenny Lin keep a storage locker so far from the city? Plus, if you look at the address, you will find that the locker is right next to the station for the local trains. I suspect that Jenny Lin, when she wanted to visit the storage locker, did not dare to take her car service, or even a taxi. I venture that she would have actually taken the train to go there, which means that the storage locker likely contains information or documents which Jenny Lin would have wanted, above all, kept a secret."

"So you want to go and have a look inside the storage locker, obviously."

"Yes. It is possible that anything of value is gone, as Tompkins will have undoubtedly pulled Jenny Lin's financial files as well. However, it is also possible that he has not gotten around to it yet. After all, he seems to have been pre-occupied with following us today."

"Why did you have to tell me this tonight? Why don't we go see what's in the storage locker tomorrow?"

Violet gave me a look in response, and my heart sunk.

"With what authority?" she asked. "We are not the police, and while I perhaps have pretended to be the police in the past to get into things, I imagine Tompkins would be especially unhappy if we decided to pretend to be MI5 agents to illegally access a storage locker."

"We're going to break into something again, aren't we?" I asked, dreading but already knowing the answer.

"Yes, we are," Violet replied.

***

"For a detective, you certainly commit a lot of crimes," I muttered as we snuck out of the back door of Violet's place in case Tompkins had agents watching the front.

"I have told you before, the art of detection and the art of the crime are very similar in many ways."

"Yeah, but did it have to be similar in the amount of time you can spend in jail for doing them?" I asked in reply.

We took the train; Violet thinking it would be far

less conspicuous. We sat across from one another, Violet silent with her eyes closed, her mouth occasionally moving slowly. I knew she was talking her way through the case, so I simply looked out the window at the lights that rushed by, where the normal people who weren't headed to an outer suburb to break into a storage locker were now doing normal people things, like settling in front of the TV or putting their kids to bed.

I had always expected that this time of night I'd be on call for emergency surgery maybe, or looking over my patient files as I got ready to do a consult on a soccer player needing an ACL repair, that sort of thing. I had never envisioned myself breaking the law, let alone doing it in a foreign country to solve a crime that MI5 had explicitly threatened to arrest us for investigating.

Still, I knew that at any time I could turn around and go back home, and yet I chose to get off the train at the Mitcham Eastfields station with Violet. I was just too curious about what was in the storage locker and who killed Jenny and Kevin Lin to say no.

Violet made me wait at the train station for a few minutes while she scoped out the area for security cameras. I was totally fine with that; if one of us screwed up and got caught on film, I was totally ok with it being her and not me. About ten minutes after she left Violet came back, telling me to make sure to stay close behind her.

The storage center was on a side street just a block or so from the train station. A medium-sized, nondescript, concrete building, it looked exactly like a million other self-storage units around the world. Unfortunately, it was surrounded by a ten-foot-high chain link fence, and floodlights abounded. I looked nervously toward the street, but Violet motioned for me to follow her. We made our way further along the fence and toward the back quickly. Violet motioned for me to hide behind a bush with her, and I did so.

"What are we waiting for?" I dared ask in a whisper.

"There is another train coming past in three minutes," Violet said. "We will wait for it to pass, then we will climb the fence. On the other side of the tracks is a grammar school; there will be no one on that property who will see us."

Sure enough, a few minutes later a train rolled past us and into the station. As soon as it left, Violet crept toward the fence. My heart racing, I followed her. Violet climbed the chain link fence like a professional, hoisting herself over the other side of it and climbing down a few feet before jumping down and landing deftly on her feet. She was surprisingly cat-like. I imagined this must not have been the first time she'd climbed a chain link fence.

If Violet resembled a cat in her elegance, my own could probably generously be compared to the elegance of a hippo. I grunted and struggled to make my way up the fence, my lack of fitness skills all too evident. There was a reason I went into medicine, and it wasn't because I'd gotten great grades in gym class back in high school.

As soon as I got to the top of the fence, I realized I was in trouble. More specifically, I had no idea how I was going to make it over to the other side. I managed to get one foot over the top, but the chain links dug in and were really painful, and I really didn't know how to get the rest of my body over safely.

"How did you get over?" I finally called out to Violet, who I was sure was down there either laughing at me or asking herself why she brought a moron like me along with her.

"Swing your second leg over as well, then crawl down until your upper body goes over also," she called back. "Also, I do not mean to rush you, but another train will be approaching in three minutes."

"What? How long between trains?"

"Ten minutes."

"How long have I taken to get up this far?"

"Five and a half minutes."

"Great," I mumbled to myself, panic beginning to rise. If I was still hanging on this fence in three minutes the slowing train would come by and someone would absolutely see us and call the cops. I didn't want to be the reason we got arrested.

I gathered my courage and swung my second leg over the top of the fence. Unfortunately, the leg of my jeans got caught on the edge of the fence, and I lost my balance. I panicked and began to fall over the other side of the fence. I heard a rip from the part of my jeans that was caught on the fence, but if anything it was a godsend as it slowed me down as my body hurtled toward the ground.

I landed with a thud, and as I groaned and looked up I saw Violet with her hand over her mouth, this time obviously trying to hide the fact that she was laughing at me.

"What? It's not my fault, I have a bad knee," I muttered, annoyed, as I struggled to get up. My knee hadn't given me the least amount of trouble then, but I was willing to throw out any excuse that might save me a little bit of dignity at this point.

Violet held out a hand and helped me up, and we made our way behind a concrete column just before the next train went by. That was a lot closer than I'd hoped for.

"I really liked those jeans," I whined as I looked at the tear that ran about six inches along the inside hem. So far, this night wasn't going too well for me.

CHAPTER 13

"Which unit number is hers?" I asked Violet as we approached the front door of the building. I noticed a security camera facing the door, about ten feet up, and also noticed that the wire connecting it to the building inside had been pulled out. How on earth Violet had gotten up there to do that, I had no idea.

"I do not know," Violet said. "I hacked their website when I found out the information, but they do not store their customer data online. It is too bad; online databases are not only easier for the business to manage, but also for me to access. We go first to the office, where we will find Jenny Lin's locker number."

At that point, I heard the lock Violet had been picking click open, and we carefully made our way into the building. I looked around, but couldn't see the white box indicating an additional security system.

"Security here isn't that great," I muttered as Violet handed me a balaclava and I put it on, along with a pair of thin gloves that matched her own.

"Self-storage places are often notorious for spending as little as possible on security," Violet told me as we made our way down the dark hallway, the light from her phone our only guide as we passed roller doors with coded keypads on the outside. "The high fence and the floodlights are designed to reduce the number of people attempting to break in, and once in they expect that the coded keypads will be enough to dissuade any potential thieves," she continued, stopping in front of a regular door marked *office*. "Here we are."

Thirty seconds later Violet had picked the lock and we were in the main office. We looked around to make sure there was no security setup here, then Violet strode toward a cabinet at the back. I held the light for her as she rustled through the documents.

"There is nothing here in Jenny Lin's name," she finally said, frustrated.

"She must be using a fake name," I mused, and Violet nodded. "Yes. Get out your phone. We will sort this pile into two, and see who has the most likely folder."

Two minutes later I found myself sitting on the floor of a self-storage space, trying to decide which name was most likely the alias used by the daughter of a UK ambassador in the storage space she possibly used to help hide evidence that she smuggled paintings for the Triads. This was definitely not the way I'd expected my life to go.

I had all the folders for people with last names from A to L.

"She definitely didn't want anyone to know she had this place if she rented it under a fake name," I said to Violet, who nodded.

We searched in silence for another minute or so, then I tried asking Violet a question.

"Hey, can I ask you something?"

"Of course."

"What would you do if you were trying to find information about someone, and you weren't getting any success looking at their social media?"

Violet looked up at me, a small smile on her face.

"Are you perhaps considering a new career in detection?" Violet asked, giving me a sly look.

"No, no, nothing like that," I said quickly. "Just... kind of helping out a friend."

"Oh yes?" Violet asked, her voice questioning. With that, I found myself telling her all about Linda and her fears that her new boyfriend wasn't telling her the truth about having siblings.

"So you see," I concluded, "I'm not really supposed to be looking into this for Linda. But I'm curious, and I thought I'd kind of give it a try. But I've pretty much stalled at the first hurdle."

"And you are discouraged because of it," Violet

deduced correctly. "Do not be! You have done more than almost everyone else in the world simply by trying. And you are not me. You have to think that I have been doing this for nearly half my life. I ask you about many medical issues because you have been doing that for nearly as long. You have your expertise, I have mine. But you should continue! You should attempt to find the answer for your friend."

"So what would you do next?" I asked.

"You have a name. I would go search birth records on the internet. Siblings are often born in the same area; see where Aaron Stone was born, and then see if anyone else with the same last name was born nearby. Alternatively, you could ask a friend by pretending to be a long-lost friend of his brother and sister's. If the person says he has no brother, but he has a sister, or vice-versa, you have your answer."

"I can't believe I didn't think of looking at the registry," I muttered. "Thank you."

"It is not a problem. And do not scold yourself too badly. You are doing well for your first case. And I must say, I am pleased that you are putting your brain to use."

I blushed slightly, thanking Violet as I continued to scroll through the large pile of files in front of me. Suddenly, I stopped at the name *Cecilia Chang*.

"Hey, Violet?"

"Yes?"

"Do you know what the last name was of Jenny's friend, Cee-Cee?"

"*Ah oui. C'était quoi?*" she muttered to herself, then two seconds later snapped her fingers. "Chang. It was Chang."

"Well I think I found the locker then, under the name Cecilia Chang."

"*Parfait*," Violet exclaimed, taking the folder from me as I started to pack up the others back into the filing cabinet. "The locker is number eighteen; we likely walked past it on the way. And as an extra bonus, the code for each locker is written in the file. It saves me from needing to figure it out myself."

Two minutes later we were standing in front of a now opened locker number eighteen. I had to admit, I was a little bit disappointed. A part of me had hoped that we would open the locker door and immediately find ourselves in front of one of the most famous paintings in the world. But unfortunately, it looked, well, surprisingly normal. There were a few cardboard boxes piled against the wall, and a couple plastic ones as well. But nothing especially stood out as being especially out of the ordinary for a place like this.

"Well, let us find out what Jenny Lin went to such lengths to hide," Violet said, making her way toward one of the boxes. I grabbed one of the plastic ones myself and opened it carefully, wondering what I was about to find. I let my imagination run wild. Maybe Jenny Lin hadn't stopped at paintings; maybe she decided to smuggle drugs on her return trips into the UK. Maybe she had filled these bags with expensive purses, and I could *borrow* one for a few days. Maybe there were bodies in here that the Triads made Jenny hide. No, that was ridiculous; we'd be able to smell decomposing bodies, easily. Of course, all of those options—except maybe the second one—were ridiculous, and I wasn't exactly surprised when I opened the box to find it was completely empty.

"There's nothing in here," I said to Violet, surprised.

"There is nothing in my box, either," Violet replied, and I had to admit I felt a bit of perverse pleasure at the sound of confusion in her voice. Violet was always so confident, so sure of herself, it was different to hear her confused.

I opened another box and once again, it was completely empty.

"This one's empty too," I said, grabbing a third, but I knew before I opened it what would be in it.

"They are all empty," Violet said. "But if MI5 had come here and emptied it, which I doubt they would as they would not have been able to find the unit in Jenny Lin's name. Nor would they have bothered to make it look nice."

"It's almost as though Jenny wanted to make it *look* like this was a normal storage unit," I muttered, half to myself.

"Yes, yes, you are right. That means there must be

something here. Something that we are missing. But what?"

Violet looked around the room, and as she did so I was suddenly reminded of something a friend of mine back in college used to do. Whenever she wanted to hide something, she would put it behind the door of her bedroom in her apartment; since the door was always open whenever someone else was in there, they would never find whatever she wanted to hide.

It was almost always pot.

I made my way to the roller door that was all the way up, reached up and just managed to grab the end of it, then pulled it down. I smiled as I saw a piece of duct tape on the other side of the wall.

"*Ah, mais* I am impressed!" Violet exclaimed as I pulled the piece of duct tape off the back of the door. On the other side of it, stuck on, was a small silver key.

"A safe deposit box key," I groaned. "Great. How are we possibly going to find what this belongs to?"

"We will find it. Look on the bright side. We did not know before that Jenny Lin had a safety deposit box. Now, we do. That is one half of the problem solved."

"The second half had better not involve more breaking and entering," I warned. "I'm drawing the line at robbing a bank."

"Well, I will keep that in mind, and hopefully things will not come to that."

CHAPTER 14

By the time we got back to Eldon Road it was nearly three in the morning. I made my way back to my little apartment, grumbled at Biscuit that he had to leave a little bit of space for me in my bed, got grumbled at by Biscuit as I moved him to the side slightly, and then promptly fell asleep.

I woke up the next morning around ten, expecting to have heard from Violet, but I didn't hear from her the whole day. By the time five pm rolled around, I texted her.

Any news on the safety deposit key? I got a reply back a minute or so later.

Nothing yet. I have no ideas yet. I will talk to you tomorrow.

I was surprised; this safety deposit key thing must have had Violet stumped. I had never seen Violet stumped before.

And yet, at nine the next morning, I got another text from Violet.

I have an idea. Come and meet me at my place.

I had a really bad feeling about Violet's "idea". However, since meeting Violet I'd broken into two places of business, had been threatened by MI5 and been held at gunpoint by a room full of Triads, and I wasn't dead or in jail yet, so maybe she knew what she was doing after all. Despite a part of my brain telling me this was a terrible idea and I absolutely shouldn't do it, I texted that I was on my way.

"You know," I told Biscuit as I fed him his breakfast and he meowed at me happily, "I'm starting to wonder if I'm not turning into a crazy person myself."

"Good morning," she greeted me when I entered the house. "I hope you are prepared for a long day; we have a lot of places to visit. I hired a car for the day; it will be here shortly. Good, you look sufficiently unlike yourself."

"What's your plan, and does it involve doing anything illegal?" Violet's hair was actually fully blonde today. "Oh my God! What did you do to your hair?"

"What do you want me to answer first? My hair is fine, it is only temporary. There will be nothing illegal. Put your mind at ease. We will simply be traveling from bank branch to bank branch in the city, and we will see what happens. Luckily for us, there has been an enormous push in the UK to get rid of safety deposit boxes. HSBC and Barclays, for example, have zero safety deposit boxes left in the whole country."

"Wow, that is big," I said, stunned. Those were two of the biggest banks in the country.

Still, Violet's plan sounded much too simple, and I couldn't see how it was going to help us figure out what bank the key belonged to, but I was sure there must be *some* sort of reasoning to Violet's madness. So when, five minutes later, a black Mercedes sedan pulled up to the curb, I followed Violet into it. She told the driver we were first going to the NatWest bank branch in Belgravia, only a few blocks from where the Lin children lived.

A few minutes later we pulled up in front of a small, white-bricked building lined with Corinthian columns, with orange bricks making up the apartment blocks above. We were right on the corner of two streets, and Violet made a show of admiring the view outside for a couple of minutes before we entered.

"I hadn't picked you as the kind of person who would appreciate a building's architecture," I noted as we walked into the lobby.

"I was simply ensuring that our friends had the opportunity to see us before we entered," Violet said.

Great. That meant MI5 were after us again. Instead of going to a counter, however, Violet simply walked up to one of the courtesy desks and played on her phone for about five minutes, then we went back into the car.

"What was that? Why didn't you do anything?"

"I told you, we are simply visiting banks. When we have reached the right one, we will know."

"How will we know?"

"You will see," Violet said slyly. We continued that way, visiting random bank branches that Violet gave the driver, for about two hours.

"*Elementary* makes the sort of thing you do look so much more interesting," I complained as we sat in the lobby of the Lloyds branch in central London.

"I recall you not even forty-eight hours ago complaining that what we were doing was illegal. I would have thought that this would be right up your alley."

"There is a healthy middle ground between committing felonies and sitting in banks all day doing nothing," I retorted. A few minutes later we left the bank and made our way back to the Mercedes, but there was a difference. Agent Tompkins was standing right there. He had the same two bulldog agents with him; at least, I thought they were the same two. To be honest they looked so much alike with their dark sunglasses, matching suits and wide stances that I couldn't be sure.

"I told you to stay away from this case, Despuis. I told you I would arrest you. I warned you. First you go to Chinatown and do… something, and now you're visiting the victim's bank? I'm arresting you on charges of perverting the course of justice." The smile on his face was that of a child who'd just seen all the presents under the tree at Christmas. I knew my face looked more along the lines of a certain Edvard Munch painting. This was it. We were going to an MI5 prison. They were probably going to put us in a cell with terrorists. If they even put us in a cell at all. What if they just took us to a black site and shot us? After all, this was the security services. They were involved in all that anti-terrorism stuff. They could do all that, couldn't they? My mind raced with possibilities, but Violet simply looked confused.

"I'm sorry," she finally replied with a perfect English accent. "I'm afraid I don't understand who, or what, you're talking about? I'm simply visiting banks in the area as a favor to my half-sister, Violet."

The two other agents glanced at each other, and even Tompkins' face fell for a moment.

"Half-sister?"

"Yes. I do not see my sister often; I have been living in Singapore for the last four years. I have come to stay in England for an extended stay with my job, however, and with the help of Violet's friend Cassie who has recently been through the same life-changing move, we have been exploring various banks."

I could tell that all three men were troubled by Violet's lie. I couldn't believe she was being so brazen. Surely there was no way this could work; just dying her hair blonde and changing the style a little bit couldn't be enough to fool three MI5 agents.

"I want proof. Show me some ID, now," Tompkins ordered, and Violet rustled through her bag. "You," he said, pointing to me. "Is she telling the truth?"

"Of course she is!" I exclaimed, trying to look realistically shocked at the question. "I can't believe you'd actually confuse a blonde woman for Violet."

Just then, Violet pulled out a UK passport and handed it to Tompkins. "There you are, I think you'll find that you've truly just made an innocent mistake. I may look like Violet, but I am very much Antonia Leicester."

Tompkins practically ripped the passport out of Violet's hands and scrutinized it. Finally, he handed it to one of the other agents. "Go to the car and run this passport, see if it comes up as legitimate," he ordered, and the man silently did as he was bidden.

"I don't believe you," Tompkins hissed. "I just don't."

"It's all right, when your man comes back with the passport you'll find that I really am who I say I am. I do look a lot like Violet though. We both take after our mother, our mutual parent."

I was worried about what would happen when the other agent came back with the passport. After all, there was no way it could be legitimate; Antonia Leicester didn't exist. I found my heart pounding as he came back from the SUV where the agents had double parked on the other side of the street. This was it. We were going to be arrested, taken to a black site and shot.

"It checks out, Sir," the man said to Tompkins. "It's a legitimate passport."

No way. How on earth had Violet pulled that off? I knew I wasn't the only person standing there wondering that.

"Arrest her anyway," Tompkins ordered.

"Um, Sir, we can't do that; we have nothing to charge her with or arrest her for."

Tompkins seethed with barely suppressed rage.

"Fine. Fine, off you go then. But you tell your 'sister'," he said, doing air quotes around the word, "that if I ever see her near this investigation, I will personally ensure she receives the maximum jail sentence possible for the crime she's been committing."

"I will Sir. And do not worry, I bear no ill-will toward your organization for the mix-up. Mistakes happen to all of us."

Tompkins practically had to be dragged back away to the waiting SUV. Violet and I got back into the Mercedes, and I gaped at her.

"What on earth just happened back there?" I asked. "Why haven't we been locked up in the Tower of London?"

Violet grinned. "We just found out where Jenny Lin's safety deposit box is," she replied. Her usual strong French accent was back.

"No, I need more details than that. Where did you get a fake passport?"

"Oh, I have a number of them at the ready in a

variety of identities, ready for when I need them, like in situations like this."

"You have got to be kidding me."

"No, not at all. It is only prudent to have a number of different identities available at all times. Sadly, I will likely have to let this one go. I will need to contact Nathan for a replacement."

"Who is Nathan?"

"My passport supplier."

"Because of course you have a passport guy. How come the passport came up as legitimate?" I had *so many questions* to ask about what had just happened.

"Nathan is very good. It is why I use him. His passports always pass muster."

"Where did the English accent come from?"

"I have lived in this country for many years, did you not think I would master the accent?"

"Well… no, I didn't really. Besides, if you're so good at it, why don't you use it all the time?"

"Because I find that people react differently when you are obviously a foreigner. And besides, this accent is more natural to me. Just because I can do an English accent does not mean I enjoy speaking that way."

"Ok, fine. What did almost getting arrested and then using a fake passport to convince the security services that you're someone else get us?"

Violet grinned at me. "That was particularly intelligent of me, I must say." At this point, I rolled my eyes at Violet's complete lack of humility. "I knew that we were being followed by MI5. And while I had Jenny Lin's credit card records, I did not know where she banked. MI5, however, would have pulled her financial information by now. They may not have looked at it in great detail as of yet, but they would know where she banked. And in a stroke of luck for us, there are in fact very few banks left in London that offer safety deposit boxes. The Lloyds branch we were just at, for example, refuses new customers. The only safety deposit boxes left belong to clients who have had them for at least four years. So we did not have too many branches to visit."

"Are you kidding me? We went to like at least fifteen other branches before we got here."

"Yes, but if safety deposit boxes were still widely available we likely would have had to visit hundreds."

Ok, things definitely could have been worse.

"So now we know where Jenny Lin banked?"

"Yes. And because safety deposit boxes are so hard to come across these days, I imagine she would not have gone elsewhere for hers. There is a very good chance that this key belongs to that box."

"How are we going to get access to it though? It's one thing to dye your hair blonde, I'm not sure even you can make yourself Asian."

"It is simpler than you might think. But unfortunately we have a larger problem than simple makeup can solve: Jenny Lin's murder has been all over the news. Someone attempting to enter her safety deposit box would look fairly suspicious, seeing as she is supposed to be dead."

"Great. So now we know where the safety deposit box is, and we have a key for it, but we can't get in."

"You are always so pessimistic. It is a problem, yes. But it is not an unsolvable problem. We will have access to the safety deposit box; I promise you that."

I had no idea how Violet intended to get access to it, but I had a feeling I didn't want to know.

CHAPTER 15

As soon as we pulled up in front of the Paddington Green police station, I had an idea of where Violet was going with this. We made our way to the second floor, which was a bustle of activity. Filled with police detectives making their way across the room, speaking with people on the phone and having discussions with coworkers, this part of the police station was always a hive of activity. We found DCI Williams, a tall man with a head of red hair, sitting at a desk filling out paperwork. When he looked up and saw Violet, I noticed a flash of worry come into his eyes.

"What has happened now?" he asked. "We haven't had any interesting cases in this district since the soup killer."

"Do not worry, I am not here to help you do your

job today. In fact, I need you to help me do mine. Also, I need you to not tell anyone else about this."

"Why not?"

"Because MI5 will arrest me if they find out."

DCI Williams leaned back in his chair and groaned. "You're involving yourself in the Lin case," he said quietly, looking around. "Come on, let's go into a private room."

DCI Williams got up from his desk and led us down the hall into one of the empty interrogation rooms. With grey walls and a simple metal table that was screwed into the floor, and a couple of metal chairs, this wasn't exactly an inviting place. DCI Williams sat on the edge of the table while I grabbed a chair and sat down. Violet stayed standing.

"So, what special hell am I in for today?" DCI Williams asked with a playful smile, and I couldn't help but smile myself. I liked DCI Williams; unlike most of the other police officers he wasn't outright hostile toward Violet, and even appreciated her help at times, but he still understood that working with her wasn't the easiest thing on the planet.

"I need you to get me a warrant," Violet said.

"Well, if I was a judge, it would be simple. Unfortunately, you know I can't just walk in and demand a warrant. What do you need a warrant for, anyway? You simply break into anywhere you need to go."

"Wait, you know she does that?" I asked, surprised.

"Of course we do. She knows we know, too. We've never caught her, but the day she is caught I know a lot of cops who will do their best to make sure she goes to jail."

"Yes, well, it will never come to that, will it? I have seen your police force work; they will never catch me." Violet put the safety deposit box key down on the table next to DCI Williams. "The problem is, I need access to this safety deposit box, and the owner is dead and has had her name on the front page of every newspaper in the country, so I cannot exactly pretend to be her and gain access that way. That is why I need the warrant."

"You know this case has been given to MI5, do you not?"

"I do, Agent Tompkins has been practically ejaculating at the thought of being able to throw me in prison."

"You really make friends everywhere you go, don't you?"

"Are you going to get me the warrant, or not? You owe me, remember? I seem to remember someone getting a commendation for their work in the Elizabeth Dalton murder."

DCI Williams sighed. "You realize blackmailing a police officer is an offence, right?"

"This is not blackmail," Violet replied with a small smile. "It's a request for a favor."

"And how exactly do you expect me to convince a

judge to give you a warrant for a crime I'm not investigating. A crime that my entire police department was removed from investigating?"

Violet shrugged. "I have given you a key with a number on it, and I can tell you it comes from the Lloyds branch at Cheapside. What you tell the judge to get into it is up to you. But I can tell you that if you tell the judge you believe the contents of the safe may be linked to the recent theft of Vermeer's Milkmaid, you would not be lying to him, and you may find yourself getting some of the credit for solving the crime as well."

DCI Williams' mouth dropped open. "How do you know about that theft? It's not hitting the papers until tonight."

"I have my reasons."

"Do you really think this murder is linked to The Milkmaid theft?" DCI Williams asked.

"I am almost certain of it."

"But how on earth did a diplomat's kid get involved?"

"That is an interesting story that involves smuggling and the Triads. I will tell you one day, perhaps. But for now, I need my warrant."

DCI Williams sighed. "I'll see what I can do. No guarantees."

"Thank you, DCI Williams. I know you will find a way. You are the least useless of all the police in this station."

"I'm not sure whether or not that was a compliment, but I'll choose to take it as one. Now get out of here, I'll call you when I have an update."

* * *

AROUND ELEVEN THE next morning I got a text from Violet. It turned out DCI Williams found a sympathetic judge, and we had our warrant. Violet hailed a cab and we met him at the Lloyds branch, where the manager, a tall, stick-thin man with white hair, met us at the front.

"We have a warrant to execute; we need to see the contents of a safety deposit box," DCI Williams told the man.

"Of course, please follow me," the man replied, leading us behind the teller stations and into the vault. DCI Williams pulled out the key that Violet had given him yesterday, and a minute later the long, thin box that had belonged to Jenny Lin was pulled out of the vault.

The manager led us with the box into a small privacy room to the side of the vault.

"I'll be waiting outside for you whenever you're ready," he said, making a discreet exit. The three of us stared at the box as Violet leaned forward and opened it.

The safety deposit box was nearly empty inside. All there was were a few folded sheets of paper, and a birth certificate. Violet carefully pulled them out of the box.

However, when Violet pulled out the sheets of paper, we realized just how important this safety deposit box really was.

There were seven rows on the piece of paper, handwritten. There were names of paintings, artists, dates, and a monetary amount next to them. The ink on the last row was darker than the others; it was obviously fresh. Jenny Lin must have come in and added it just before her death.

The Milkmaid—Vermeer—May 7th—£200,000

It was by far the largest sum of money on the sheet; the first couple only netted her around twenty thousand pounds, but then the third and fifth paintings netted her fifty thousand, the fourth one hundred thousand and the sixth seventy thousand. If the dates represented when Jenny received the paintings, which seemed logical enough, it meant she had been smuggling for the Triads for a little over a year.

The other papers all had names and artists as well. There was one Picasso, and a Rafael, along with a few others by artists whose names I didn't recognize.

"What are those?" DCI Williams asked, reading over Violet's shoulder.

"They are a list of paintings that were stolen by the United Dragons gang of Triads and smuggled into Taiwan by Jenny Lin," Violet replied.

"So you weren't lying to me yesterday when you said she was involved in that?" DCI Williams asked.

"No, I was telling you the truth."

"How does this help you find the painting, or the person who killed Jenny Lin, or whatever else it is you're up to?"

"It is information. Information is always helpful. I do not know yet how this will help me find the murderer. But it cannot hurt." Violet took her phone out and snapped a quick photo of the list. "This way, if Agent Tompkins ever manages to figure out this box exists, the contents will still be untouched," she explained. "Just because I am better than MI5 does not mean I play dirty; I leave all the clues I can for him to find."

Violet placed the list of paintings down on the table next to the box and unfolded the other sheet of paper. This one seemed to be a more detailed version of the last one. It seemed that Jenny Lin kept fairly detailed records of everything she smuggled. Unfortunately for us, they were all in code. The code referencing the last painting was obvious from the same recent, darker ink.

Received phone call from LW to pick up Ji. Changeover complete at GS, 7/May. LHR to TPE via HKG 8/Jun, meeting W at MO1629

Then, scribbled quickly underneath was another note. *LW meeting at BS 10/May 22.*

"The tenth of May, that was the night that Jenny and Kevin Lin were killed, right?" I asked.

"Yes," Violet said quietly. "It seems as though Jenny

Lin had a meeting with someone with the initials 'LW' the night she was killed."

We looked at each other. I knew we both instantly knew who had those initials.

CHAPTER 16

"Those initials obviously stand for Lin Wei, don't they?" I asked Violet when we were back in her apartment. She went to her computer in the corner of the study and uploaded the pictures she had taken of Jenny Lin's papers to print them out. Instead of immediately agreeing with me as I expected though, she shrugged.

"It is possible. But there are other possibilities as well."

"Fine. Would you say it's *likely* that Lin Wei went to meet Jenny the night that she died?"

"Likely? Yes, I think I would say it was likely."

"How are we going to figure out what the rest of the code says, though?" I asked.

"Well, I already have much of it figured out."

"Really? Damn, all I could figure out was that she

was meeting with someone named LW the night she was killed."

"Not only the night she was killed, but more specifically, at ten o'clock at night. The twenty-two after the date I am certain represents the time. In Europe, we still use twenty-four hour time regularly, because we are not savages."

Ignoring the jab at America, I asked another question. "What about the line above it? What can you make of that?"

"Jenny received a phone call from someone to pick up... Ji. I do not know what that part is, but I can assume it was the painting. If you read the lines above, you will see that LW always calls her to pick up a painting. They complete the changeover somewhere, GS. I do not know where that is either. There is a Goodge Street underground station in Camden, and Great Portland Street in Westminster, but I am not certain that is correct. I believe Jenny has put everything in code. Regardless, I believe Jenny received the painting on May 7th, three days before she was killed. The plan was, as Lin Wei told us, for them to wait a few weeks for the furor over the theft to die down, and then to smuggle the painting out of the country. In this case, it seems Jenny had planned to visit Taiwan, via Hong Kong, in June. LHR, TPE and HKG are airport codes."

"And the last part?" I asked, very impressed with what Violet had managed to glean from what mainly just seemed to be random letters to me.

"I expect that the plan is for her to meet a man whom she has coded 'M' someplace—I do not know what MO1629 means, although I suspect 1629 would be a hotel room number, and MO perhaps 'Mandarin Oriental', one of the biggest luxury hotels in Taipei. That would be where she would have gone to drop the painting off with the Triads, and from there Jenny Lin's involvement was ended."

I looked at the list of coded information Jenny had left. "It seems like this last time was the only time she ever had another meeting with LW, apart from when he did the changeover."

"Yes," Violet said. "While I am not certain, I imagine this LW is in fact, the murderer. I also would not be surprised if he has the painting; if Jenny Lin had not kept it at her home, she would have left it either in her storage locker or her safety deposit box."

"So if we find the murderer, we also find the missing painting?" I asked.

"I suspect that may be the case. Or at the very least, we find the murderer and we find *who* has the painting. It may still be difficult to find *where* they have put it, if they have not already sold it on."

"What are we going to do now?" I asked.

"Now, we are going to speak to the one person who has the information we need. In fact, I believe this might be him now; I texted him to come by here earlier."

The doorbell rang suddenly, and Violet got up and

made her way to the door. When she came back, she was joined by Lin Wei.

"Ah, Cassie. It is nice to get to see you again," Lin Wei said to me, bowing slightly.

"And you as well," I replied, although I didn't mean it. I was fairly sure he didn't mean his words, either.

Violet excused herself and Lin Wei and I sat in silence. I had no idea what to say to the man; I couldn't believe the leader of a major Triad gang was sitting right in front of me. A moment later Violet thankfully returned, with a tray of tea, which she carefully poured for Lin Wei, and then poured a cup for me as well.

"So, Violet, what is it that has happened that requires me to come to your home? It is a lovely home, of course, and I am honored to be here, but I thought I had told you everything you needed to know when you came to visit me at my place of work."

"Oh, trust me, Lin Wei, you absolutely want to hear what I have to tell you. You are about to become the prime suspect in Jenny Lin's murder."

If Lin Wei was surprised by Violet's statement, he didn't show it. However, her brown eyes bored into him; I knew she was taking in every detail of his reaction.

"Well, in that case, someone is about to make a mistake."

"I do not necessarily think you are lying. That is why I have invited you here. I need to know more details about the process behind the art thefts. If you help me, there is a good chance that you will not be prosecuted. If you do not, you will be arrested. They will try you, and believe me, they will likely win. Jenny Lin was keeping notes on all of the paintings that you had got her to smuggle for you, did you know that?"

This time Lin Wei did raise an eyebrow slightly. "I did not know, no."

"And her notes also specified a lot of information regarding the transaction. In fact, her notes mention a meeting with someone with the initials LW on the night of her death."

This time Lin Wei's eyes widened; he was noticeably shocked.

"I am telling you, Violet. I am a man of my word. I did not kill Jenny Lin. I do not know who LW could be, but I swear to you, it was not me. I was nowhere near her that night."

"I don't know," Violet told him. "After all, what if Jenny called the meeting? What if she wanted to get out of the smuggling game, but you would not let her? What if you killed her so that she would not tell the police what she had been doing for your organization?"

Lin Wei shook his head forcefully. "No, no, that did not happen."

"I am not saying that I believe you. But I need to ask more questions. I need details about the transfer of the paintings, and who is involved."

"If I tell you, it ruins my whole operation," Lin Wei

said, holding his arms out. "You will be able to tear it to bits."

"Your entire operation is already torn to bits. Your smugglers are dead. And if you do not tell me, you will almost certainly spend the rest of your life in jail," Violet said. Her voice was hard; she was completely serious.

The two of them stared at each other for a couple of minutes, then Lin Wei broke. With a sigh, he dropped his head to his chin and closed his eyes.

"Fine. You are correct, of course. I would rather give up a small slice of my business than my freedom."

"I knew you were not a stupid man. You have made the correct choice."

Lin Wei took a moment to think about what he was going to say, and then began to explain the operation to us.

"We have a contact who tells us about paintings that are of various difficulties to steal. This contact is not Triad; however he is a man that I worked with in Hong Kong for a number of years."

"English?"

"Yes, he lived in Hong Kong back when it was still owned by England. He was the most skilled white man I have ever seen in the art of Kung Fu. A skill that came in handy for me a few times, I must say. After the handover he moved back to England, but he still had his fingers in a few pies, as the English say. I reached out to him when I moved here ten years ago, and he has been supplying me with that information ever since. I pay him fairly."

"The Milkmaid is worth enough that paying someone fairly is not always enough," Violet murmured. "But pray, continue."

"Our thief himself is Triad. I will not tell you who it is, obviously, but let it be known that I trust him implicitly."

"It is your son, Zhang Wei," Violet said.

"You cannot know that," Lin Wei hissed.

"About a year ago," Violet started, "I happened upon your son in a small gallery in London. His movements might have been too subtle for the gallery owner to notice, but they were not subtle enough to fool *me*," she said, her eyes glimmering. "I knew then your son was an art thief."

Lin Wei's face blanched slightly. "Why did you not turn him in to the police?"

Violet shrugged. "I was working a far more important case at the time. And besides, there was no crime. It was simply the way he looked at the gallery, I recognized the signs of a man who steals art."

"I thank you for your discretion," Lin Wei muttered. "I shall not confirm your theory. But I do trust our thief completely."

I wondered briefly if Zhang Wei might have wanted to take his father's spot in the Triads. Framing him for murder would certainly be one way to get his father out of the way. Lin Wei continued his explanation just then, however, and I turned my focus back to that.

"Our thief would then take the painting in a tote bag, and hand it off to Jenny Lin at Charing Cross station. He would enter one of the photo booths and leave. Jenny Lin was to come past five minutes later and retrieve the package. I always had two men watching to ensure both that Jenny Lin did not arrive early to see the thief, and to make sure that the thief did not linger to see who the smuggler was. They were also to ensure that no one else used the photo machine. The two men are my most trusted; the only two I would give such an assignment to."

"So your thief and Jenny Lin never saw each other?"

"No," Lin Wei said, shaking his head.

"Which means the only people who knew that Jenny would be in possession of the painting were you, and the two men that you trust implicitly."

"I not only trust them implicitly, I was with them when Jenny and Kevin Lin were killed. They could not have done it."

Violet frowned to herself. "The thief had to have figured out who had the painting somehow," she muttered to herself.

"I honestly cannot tell you how it was figured out," Lin Wei said, shaking his head slowly. "Our organization was designed so that as few people as possible knew about each other."

"If I have more questions, I will text your prepaid

mobile. Are you still using the eight-three-nine number?"

"I am," Lin Wei replied, getting up. "Thank you for the wonderful cup of tea, and the conversation. I will see within my ranks if I can dig up any information for you. The loss of Jenny and Kevin, it was… profound, to my organization. We want justice as much as you do."

"I would appreciate you letting me know as soon as possible if you find anything," Violet said, and the two of us stood up.

"Miss Cassie, it was nice to see you again," Lin Wei said to me, bowing slightly, and I replied in kind as Violet took him to the front door. When she came back, she was deep in thought.

"This is turning out to be much more interesting a challenge than even I had expected," she said. That certainly didn't sound good.

CHAPTER 17

I decided to spend most of the day with Violet, doing my little part in trying to solve the puzzle. I brought Biscuit over, who decided he very much enjoyed sitting on the top of Violet's bookcase and looking down on Violet and I as we each did our own thing. Violet texted so many people it was a wonder she didn't suffer from carpal tunnel syndrome. Every few minutes or so I heard the familiar bing of her phone indicating she had received another message.

For myself, I spent most of my time sorting through every single credit card purchase Jenny Lin had made over the past year. If I could find something out of the ordinary, maybe that could get us on the right track. But unfortunately for me, there were only purchases from luxury boutiques, a bit of online shopping, and a whole bunch of money spent at clubs, and cafés near the London School of Economics. She also spent way more money than I could have possibly imagined at JustEat, a local London food delivery service.

I was getting frustrated when Violet suddenly let out an exclamation of pleasure.

"*Ah mais oui!* That must be it. Cassie, do you believe in coincidence?"

"Yes, of course," I said.

"If I told you that every painting that was stolen was insured by the same company, would you think that was a coincidence?"

"I definitely wouldn't," I replied. "There were seven paintings. That's more than a coincidence."

"*Exactement*," Violet replied. "I think it is as well. Atkinson Insurance is the company that has insured all of the products."

"Hm, that's funny," I said. "The third victim in the explosion worked for an insurance company. I don't know which one though."

"What did you just say?" Violet said, practically pouncing on me.

"Um, the third victim… what was his name… Green-something. He worked for an insurance company."

"*Merde!* I have been an *imbécile!*" Violet paced around the room, her hands behind her back.

She turned to me suddenly. "How did you know about the insurance man?"

"Ummm, I spoke to Brianne, my friend who works

at the hospital. She was there that night when he got brought in and spoke to his wife."

"Call her, now. Tell her to come here. I need to speak with her. I need to know everything she knows."

I took out my phone and texted Brianne.

Hey, you wanted to meet Violet? She needs to meet you too. Needs to know everything you know about Andrew Greenhouse. I got a reply back a moment later.

Ooooh, is it about the murder?

It is, yeah.

I'm working right now. I can be over there in three hours?

I relayed Brianne's message back to Violet. "Tell her that if she arrives here in twenty minutes I'll give her one thousand pounds," Violet replied.

"Seriously?"

"Seriously."

I texted Brianne and got a message back a second later.

Seriously?

Yup, I replied, sending her the address.

That's definitely a deal then! See you soon!

Fifteen minutes later Brianne was knocking on the front door. I went to let her in and gave her a quick hug when I saw her.

"Hey," Brianne said, looking past me into Violet's home. "I managed to convince Lenny to cover the rest of my shift for me. Worst case scenario I was totally going to quit, a grand is like, two months' worth of working at Chipotle," she told me.

"Yeah, good call," I replied, leading her into the study, where Violet came forward and shook her hand.

"Hello," she said. "It is nice to meet you. I have been told you have spoken with Andrew Greenhouse."

"I did, yeah," Brianne told her. "Well, I only spoke with him briefly, yesterday, and the night of the accident. I did speak with his wife for a little while on the night of the explosion though, and a couple of times since."

"Tell me everything the wife told you, and everything Greenhouse himself told you. Please. It's very important," Violet said, motioning toward the couch. "And please, sit. You must be tired, having been at the hospital all day before going straight to work."

Brianne looked at me, confused. "I didn't tell you about the shift at the hospital."

"Yeah, she does that," I told Brianne. "It's basically magic."

"It is not magic, it is simply that I *observe*. Brianne mentioned that she was at her job, yet there is a faint aroma of hospital grade cleaning fluid coming off her. And as a doctor in training, she would be used to being on her feet, yet she looked at the couch as one looks at a lover one hasn't seen in a long time."

I was worried Brianne would be insulted, but instead she just burst out laughing.

"My God! Cassie was not joking when she said you

were magic. Sorry about the smell. And for your information, yes, I would absolutely make love to this couch right now, as long as it did all the work. But as I'm not an exhibitionist, and you're both here, I'll have to take a rain check," she said, stroking the leather seductively. I laughed as Brianne continued. "I spoke with Andrew Greenhouse for a little while yesterday. He was very badly out of sorts, I must say. They're keeping him heavily sedated, and nothing he said made any sense. He kept mumbling about how it was too early. They've been reducing the amount of sedative they're giving him though. He should be awake now."

"Too early?" I asked, and Brianne shrugged.

"I don't know what he meant by that at all."

"And he said nothing else?" Violet asked.

"Nothing coherent," came Brianne's reply. "The night of the accident he asked me if anyone had been killed in the explosion and I told him about the two Lin children. He seemed quite sad about it."

"What about his wife?"

"I saw Andrew Greenhouse's wife the night he came in, and a few times since then. She was fraught with worry. She said they lived on Cadogan Lane, and that he was walking home from work and got caught in the explosion. He had texted her before he left, telling her he was picking up dinner from Shakespeare's Head, a nearby pub that he often brought food back home from."

"And he works for Atkinson Insurance?" Violet asked.

"His wife didn't say, but she mentioned that the office he worked at was in Holborn, if that helps?"

Violet's eyes lit up suddenly.

"Oh yes, that does help. You say they lived on Cadogan Lane?"

"Yes. That's the address listed on his chart, and his wife's emergency contact as well."

"And you are one hundred percent certain that he worked in Holborn? She definitely didn't say Hammersmith, or something else?"

"Just because I'm Australian doesn't automatically make me a moron," Brianne told Violet, causing me to smile. "I know the difference between Holborn and Hammersmith. I am one hundred percent sure she said Holborn. Why?"

Violet got up and began to pace around. "Because Andrew Greenhouse is a double murderer, and an art thief. Was there anything else the wife told you?"

"Umm… yeah, a few days later she told me her husband had been working on a big deal at work, which was why he was working late. She said he was really looking forward to that deal, but that it was high risk. She also said that he was a good man, and that they were planning on having kids next year. Why do you think he's a murderer?"

"Anything else?"

"No, that's all I can think of."

"That is all right. Already you have given me the proof I needed. Andrew Greenhouse killed both Lin children. The question is, where is the painting?"

"What painting?" Brianne asked, looking at me, confused.

"The Milkmaid, by Vermeer," I replied. "Turns out the Lin kids were smuggling paintings, and Violet thinks that whoever killed them took the painting."

"Wait, that painting that's been in the news? The super expensive one?" Brianne asked, but Violet had moved on.

"He *must* have taken the painting," Violet said. "It is the only explanation that makes any sense at all!"

"How do you know he did it? What about Holborn tipped you over the edge on that?" I asked Violet. I was as curious about that as Brianne.

"The trains!" Violet exclaimed. "The trains, they do not make sense!"

"He took the tube from work? What's wrong with that? It was before one am, they were all still running."

"Yes, but he took the *wrong* train," Violet said, moving to her desk and unfolding a large map of the London Underground. Because of course she had one just lying around.

"See here? He lived on Cadogan Lane, halfway between the Sloane Street and Knightsbridge stations. But he worked in Holborn. The Piccadilly line goes directly from the Holborn Underground station to Knightsbridge Station. If he had done that, he would have got home without going as far as Bourne Street, and he never would have been near the explosion zone. To get to Sloane Street, he would have had to take the Piccadilly Line to Gloucester Station, then transferred to either the Circle or District line to get to Sloane Street. But in doing that, he would have had to pass Knightsbridge station, so he would have made his commute longer. There was no reason for him to be at Sloane Street station whatsoever."

"So him telling his wife he was at work and coming home was a lie," I reasoned.

"Yes. And if he had food from the pub local to his work, then he definitely did come from there."

"I don't know," I said slowly. "I'm not sure if you can convict someone for murder based on them taking a less sensible train route home."

"It is enough! It is enough that I know. Now that I know who to look at, I will find the proof to convict him. I will find the painting. Thank you, Brianne. You have been instrumental in solving a murder. Let me get you the cash I promised you."

Violet made her way to the bookcase, grabbed a random book, opened it and pulled out a handful of twenty pound notes.

"This should be one thousand," Violet said. "Thank you again for your help."

Brianne thanked Violet for the cash and stood up. "Well, I can't say I understood everything that happened here tonight, but I'm going to go home and sleep, then Cassie what do you say we go for a drink and you can explain to me what just happened."

"Deal," I said with a grin.

"By the way," Violet called out, "You should call your sister. She worries about you."

Brianne stared at Violet for a second, then shook her head. "It really is magic," she said. "Text me if you need a hand with anything," she told me.

"Thanks," I told Brianne, giving her another quick hug before closing the door after her. When I turned back around, Violet was practically giddy.

"We know who our murderer is now. We are in the end stages of this investigation. Come! This is when things get interesting."

If everything that had happened so far was Violet's definition of boring, I wasn't sure I wanted to see what she considered interesting.

CHAPTER 18

I left Violet soon afterwards as she wanted to think her way through the case.

"There is only one problem," I said. "Where is the painting?"

"Ah yes, that is a problem indeed. If we can find the painting, we will have all of the proof we will need. I must figure out where the painting is hidden. I will text you when I have a plan."

So that was how I found myself that afternoon, playing with Biscuit for a while, trying to find something to distract my brain that didn't have anything to do with murder. Eventually I took out my iPad and began to browse birth record websites.

I wasn't expecting much. After my total failure at e-stalking Aaron Stone's social media accounts, I had more or less resigned myself to never finding any answers for Linda, despite the pep talk Violet had given me. Still, there was a part of me that wanted to give it a shot. After all, Violet recommended this option, and she knew what she was doing, right?

I found an engine to search birth records in the UK, and started off by typing in the surname 'Stone' and nothing else. Unfortunately, that got me hundreds of thousands of results. That certainly wasn't going to help. When I narrowed it down to 'Aaron Stone' I was left with only around one thousand results. That was more manageable. Looking at dates of birth, I was able to narrow down the list to about two hundred people in the right age group.

I stared at the list, wondering how to narrow it down further, when suddenly I remembered something. I opened up Aaron Stone's Facebook page again and scrolled down. There was one public post, made a few months earlier, on February 18th, from one of his friends, wishing him a happy birthday.

I grinned at my own ingenuity. Maybe I wasn't so terrible at this as I thought. I scrolled through my list and found one Aaron Stone, born February 18th, 1982. That would make him thirty-four years old, which seemed about right. That had to be the correct Aaron Stone. His place of birth was listed as Ipswich.

I did another search, this time looking for anyone else with the last name Stone who was born at Ipswich hospital.

Unfortunately, there were only two of them. One was six months old, and the other nearly ninety.

"Damn it," I said, angrily tossing my iPad aside; Biscuit taking advantage of the free spot on my legs to stretch across me and beg for belly rubs. I could feel the negative thoughts sneaking back into my brain. Of course I wasn't good enough to do this. This was what Violet did, not me. I was never going to find an answer for Linda. How stupid of me to even try.

I started to burrow myself under the blankets again. I could feel the energy seeping out of me. Maybe I could sleep for a while. Biscuit wasn't going to need his dinner for another few hours, at least. Violet would eventually call about the painting, I could get out of bed then.

No, I eventually thought. *You can't keep doing this. You can find a way to solve this. You have a fricking medical degree, finding out if someone has siblings should be a thousand times easier than figuring out where the nuclei of each individual cranial nerve is located after you've been awake for thirty straight hours.*

I groaned as my brain forced me to get up once more. I knew it was good for me; I'd spent way too much of the past few months lying in bed feeling as though I didn't even have the energy to be awake.

But how was I going to do it? Suddenly, I had an idea. It was a terrible, terrible idea, with a good chance of backfiring. But something Violet told me a few months earlier had stuck in my brain. She had told me I should practice lying when it didn't matter, because no one would know, and if they did realize, they wouldn't care.

That was how Brianne and I had become friends; I had used her as my first test subject, and it went, well, pretty badly. But Violet was right. If you lied to people you didn't know, it didn't matter if they caught you.

I grabbed my iPad and opened up Aaron Stone's Facebook page again. I had been going about this all wrong. I didn't need to know what Aaron's life was all about, I needed to find one of his friends.

The friend who had wished Aaron a happy birthday was named Stephen Shaw. I clicked on his profile, much of which was private, but I did notice that he worked at a book store in Bloomsbury, London's best known shopping district. I looked at the clock; it would still be open for another two hours. I had plenty of time to make my way to the shop before it closed and see if Stephen was working there.

As I took the underground toward the shop, I hashed out the details of my plan in my brain. It wasn't just so that I wouldn't screw it up; I also knew if I wasn't thinking about exactly what to do I was absolutely going to wuss out of going through with this plan. I had always been a good girl. I was the girl in elementary school who told the teacher when she added up my test results wrong in my favor. I definitely wasn't the girl who went into central London pretending to be somebody else to find out the truth about an acquaintance's hunch that someone was lying to them. And yet, here I was.

When I got to Bloomsbury I realized I was actually right next to Holborn, where Andrew Greenhouse worked. I put the thought out of my head as I made my way down Bury Place and found the London Review Bookshop.

I stopped as I passed a corner store on the way there and noticed the headlines:

Vermeer Masterpiece Stolen
The Milkmaid Disappears in England
The Art Theft of the Century
Netherlands Angry: Art Theft

It looked as though the news of the Vermeer being stolen had finally hit the news. It was funny to read the headlines, knowing I was actually involved in the case to get the paintings back, and that I knew so much more than the newspapers did. I had never been in that situation before. Still, I wasn't here to think about the gas explosion in Belgravia, I was here for my own answers. I continued down Bury place until I found the right place.

The London Review Bookshop looked incredibly classy from the outside; the wooden green façade was trimmed with gold, and plain gold lettering at the top advertised the name of the business. The display books in the window advertised older editions of classic books and hidden treasures, rather than the latest airport thrillers. I made a mental note to come back here another time; this seemed like the sort of place where people really *knew* books.

I entered the store and found myself greeted by a man who was obviously Stephen Shaw; he looked exactly like the profile picture on his Facebook page.

"Hello there," he greeted me. "Can I help you find anything today?"

"Hi," I said, flashing him a smile. "Sorry, I'm just wondering if you're Stephen Shaw," I asked.

He looked a bit confused, but nodded. "I am, yes. Is anything wrong?"

"No no, not at all," I answered. "It's just that I moved to America a number of years ago and lost touch with an old friend. I was looking for her, and someone mentioned that they knew you, that you worked here and that you were friends with her brother, Aaron?"

Stephen's face suddenly fell. "Yes. Yes, of course. Aaron's sister." My heart swelled. I had figured it out! I was totally there! "I'm afraid Fiona went through some bad times. She's in prison, actually. Holloway, I believe. Until they close that prison, anyway."

"Oh," was all I could reply. I was stunned. That explained everything, didn't it? Aaron telling Linda he didn't have any siblings, but being evasive about it. I imagined he'd rather pretend his sister didn't exist.

"I imagine they have visiting hours, if you'd still like to see her," Stephen told me.

"Thank you for telling me," I replied, trying to look like the news was shocking and saddening, and I practically ran out of the bookstore. As I took the train back to my basement suite, I felt a profound feeling of satisfaction for the first time in a long time. I'd had a problem to solve, all on my own, and I'd solved it. It was hard, and I almost gave up a couple of times, but in the end I persevered and I made it through. And I was also fairly certain that Stephen Shaw had no idea I wasn't who I said I was.

As soon as I got back home I typed the name "Fiona Stone" into my iPad. Thanks to a couple of old newspaper articles, I found out that a year earlier Fiona Stone had broken into three homes and stolen jewellery, and had finally been caught. It seemed that she had pled guilty to the offenses, and was sentenced to two years at Holloway Prison.

"Look at that, Biscuit. Maybe I'm not completely hopeless at this after all," I said to my cat as he pounced onto a little felt mouse sitting on the floor. Next time I saw Linda, I was finally going to be able to answer her question. I'd done some investigative work all on my own—granted, with some input from Violet—and I'd solved my case! I was surprised at how much pride I felt in myself. Maybe it was time for me to stop moping around and find something else to do with my own life for a little while, I thought to myself.

CHAPTER 19

The following day, around eleven in the morning, I got a text from Violet.

Come to my house. We are going to find a stolen painting today.

I did as Violet asked and ten minutes later we were standing in front of the entrance to Sloane Street underground station.

"So what are we doing here?" I asked.

"We are going to find a painting," Violet replied.

"And how exactly are we going to do that?" Sometimes trying to get information out of Violet was like pulling teeth.

"I have no idea," Violet replied.

"You realize it's raining, right? I could be indoors, watching Netflix right now."

"You have an umbrella, you have nothing to complain about," Violet replied. "Besides, this is far more interesting than anything on the *television*," she said, practically spitting out that last word. I had a feeling Violet wasn't a fan of Supernatural or Game of Thrones.

"So do we stand here and wait for the painting to find us?" I asked. "What's the plan?"

"We are going to walk through Belgravia. Walk me through the timeline of the crime," Violet said, motioning to a bench that was hidden under cover well enough that we wouldn't get rained on.

"Well," I started, closing my umbrella, "Jenny Lin has an appointment with Andrew Greenhouse."

"Yes."

"He goes to her house at nine pm. They argue, presumably over the painting, and he kills her. Still agreed?"

"Yes."

"Jenny Lin is dead, Andrew Greenhouse pulls the gas line from the back of the stove. He takes the painting, and leaves."

"Yes."

I had to think about the next bit for a little while before I came up with it. "Oh! Andrew Greenhouse stayed to make sure that Kevin Lin came home and blew up the house before noticing his sister was dead and sounding the alarm, but he didn't get far enough away from the blast and was caught up in it!"

"While I agree that this is what happened, you are forgetting one thing. What happened to the painting?"

I sat in silence for a minute before the answer came to me. "Well, it had to be destroyed?"

Violet shook her head. "No, that is the thing. It would not have been destroyed. Andrew Greenhouse was injured, yes. But the description of his injuries imply that he had the house fall on him, not that he was burned, do they not?"

"Yeah, that's what Brianne said."

"So in that case, the painting would be *damaged*, yes. But it would not be destroyed completely. There would have been evidence of the painting found near the body, and I guarantee you that had that sort of thing appeared we would have heard about it by now."

"That means the painting wasn't near Andrew Greenhouse when the house exploded," I said. "But where could he have put it? It had to be somewhere near here, and he couldn't have gone home, or his wife would have mentioned it."

"*Précisement!* Andrew Greenhouse killed Jenny Lin, then set up the gas leak. He then left the house with the painting. He stored it somewhere, and returned to ensure both Lin children were killed, intending to return afterwards and take the painting back home. He must have thought it more prudent to hide the painting until he knew both Lin children were killed, in case Kevin survived the explosion and he had to kill him by hand. However, for some reason, Andrew Greenhouse was too close to the blast and found himself the unwitting victim."

"Which means that the painting he hid has to still be hidden where he left it, because he's been sedated in a hospital bed until a couple of days ago, and there's no way that he'd trust that sort of thing to someone else."

"Exactly. You do not tell even your wife that you have stolen one of the world's most valuable paintings, especially when no one else knows where it is. If he has hidden it well enough, he will assume that it will not be found until he is recovered and can retrieve it himself."

"And that's why we're here, we have to try and figure out where he would have hidden it," I said slowly, understanding.

"*Oui, exactement*," Violet said, nodding. "Andrew Greenhouse was not wearing gloves when he was found; I asked the policeman who had been in charge of the case previously. It means that if we manage to find the painting, it will have Andrew Greenhouse's fingerprints on it. We will be able to prove he is the murderer, and a thief."

"Ok," I said. "So what are we looking for?"

"Anything that looks as if a person could hide something. It does not have to be big; the painting was quite small. It does, however, have to be secure," Violet said as we began walking up Cliveden Place, a commercial street only a couple blocks away from the explosion. "We sadly cannot visit Bourne Street itself at the moment; I imagine that Agent Tompkins would love to find us near the scene of the crime. However, we are permitted to shop in Belgravia."

Next to an upscale homewares store was a large, somewhat secluded space, but Violet clucked when I mentioned it.

"No, no, no. It is all wrong. He would have left the painting somewhere that would have been *completely* safe. This is too exposed. It cannot be here." We continued to make our way through the streets. Violet's eyes darted from side to side as she searched for somewhere suitable.

"What if he had a lover or someone who lives near here?" I asked. "Then we'd never find it."

"Do not say never! He may have, but we do not yet know. We must exhaust this method, first."

"I'm definitely starting to feel exhausted," I muttered to myself. Not to mention I was getting wet, and I was hungry. I looked up and saw the closest thing to a miracle I'd ever seen. There was a pub directly in front of us! Called The Antelope, the exterior was dark brown paneled wood, with flowers above the black sign indicating the name in gold lettering. The apartments around it were all white, and it stood out in the middle of the street. I wondered if I could convince Violet to eat here.

I turned to look at her, but her face had taken on that look she got when she was thinking. She was looking directly ahead, her fingers drumming against her leg. I let her think for a bit, and as her eyes began to sparkle with delight I asked her what it was.

"This is it!" she said.

"What's it?"

"This place. We must go in and eat."

"Wow, this place truly is a miracle," I said, heading for the door. As soon as I stepped inside the warmth hit me like suddenly being enveloped in a warm blanket. The place was small and cozy; a couple were seated at a small table off to the side of the bar, and a group of friends were obviously having a late lunch at one of the two larger tables right by the bar. Violet and I settled ourselves at a small round table on the far side of the bar, and I set my coat down and asked Violet what she wanted before going up to the bar to order.

"I'll have the Chicken Caesar Salad, no dressing, and a glass of water please," Violet asked me. I went up and placed her order, along with a Chalcroft Farm Beef Burger and a beer for myself. I hadn't spent two hours walking around in the rain to eat a salad.

I made my way back to our table and sat down across from Violet. "So why are we here?"

"What was missing from the crime scene?" Violet asked in reply.

"Ummm… the painting?"

"No, we have already deduced that it was hidden. What should have been at the crime scene, and wasn't?"

"I don't know," I replied, completely confused.

"The food!" Violet replied. "Think! You are Andrew Greenhouse. You are hiding from your wife the fact that you are going to steal a painting and kill the person keeping it. You do not want her to get suspicious, so you tell her that you have picked up dinner from the place near your work where you always eat. However, if he had actually done that, what would have happened?"

"The food would have been cold by the time he actually got home," I replied.

"Yes! So he has to get new food. The Inn of Court, it is a Fuller's pub. They are a chain."

"Oh!" I said, realizing suddenly. "The food from here and from there would have been the same!"

"Exactly. If Andrew Greenhouse left his work, got the food and went home, it would still be warm. So he killed Jenny Lin, took the painting, and he came here."

The waitress came by with our food just then and placed it in front of us. My mouth watered as I looked at the burger; I had absolutely earned this by wandering around in the rain for like, two hours, and I ignored Violet's look of scorn as she took a bite of what I was certain was an incredibly unsatisfying salad.

"Excuse me," Violet told the waitress before she left. "You wouldn't happen to have been working the night of the explosion, were you?"

"Ohhh, yes, I was," the waitress answered. "Bad night, that one. Those poor people. I'm glad one of them is going to be all right. He was just in a few minutes before the explosion, too."

"Oh was he?" Violet asked, her eyes gleaming.

"Yes, he said he wanted to bring some food home to his wife. Ordered a burger and fish and chips to go, then he went to use the loo, went back out and told me he'd be back in a little bit to pick up his food. He left and never came back. About fifteen minutes later the explosion happened; we heard it from here. It was bloody terrifying, I must say."

"Did he have anything with him?" Violet asked. "The man, I mean."

"Oh yes, he did. A shopping bag, from Harrods. I figured he'd just had a long day at the office and stopped to get something for his wife as an apology to go with the late supper."

"Thanks," Violet told her, taking out her phone while I munched on a hot, crispy French fry.

"Who are you texting?" I asked.

"DCI Williams," Violet told me. "He'll be here shortly, we can eat our meal until then."

I was amazed at the detachment Violet was able to manage while we ate our food. "So I see that you have solved your problem of your friend's boyfriend and the lie he told her?"

The fry that was halfway to my mouth paused in midair. "How could you *possibly* know that?" I asked. There was no way. She couldn't know. She had to be guessing.

"You went out yesterday afternoon. You never go out, unless it's with the cat, or to get food. You looked far too thoughtful to be going to get food, which means you were doing something important to you. You are still depressed; you do not do much on your own, so it must have been that. When you came back an hour later, you walked with more confidence; you were obviously a lot happier. I took that to mean that you had found a solution to your problem."

I shook my head slowly. "I'm not sure what part of that is more insane. The fact that you actually figured out where I was going, what I was doing, and what the result was based on my body language when I left the apartment and came back or the fact that you were spying on me."

"I was not spying on you," Violet said. "I was watching the street."

"I have never, not once, seen the front blinds that look onto the street open. I swear you're sneakier than Biscuit sometimes."

"I do not look physically. I have cameras. You have seen my line of work; it would be imprudent not to have extensive home security. Besides, in that particular situation, I was simply reviewing tapes to see if Agent Tompkins had been past or not."

"Does that really make things better though?" I asked.

"Are you going to tell me what you discovered, or not?"

Realizing that Violet was never going to understand just how creepy watching tapes of people going down her street really was, I told her about my trip to the bookstore and how I found out that Aaron Stone did have a sister, she was simply incarcerated for at least another year.

"Excellent!" Violet said, clapping her hands happily when I told her about it. "You are taking initiative! You are doing things! It is good for you. I am glad that you did this."

Violet looked like she was going to say something more, but just then DCI Williams came in through the door and walked over to us.

"You do realize that I'm not working the Lin murders, right?" he asked Violet, giving me a smile and a nod of hello, which I returned.

"Of course," Violet replied. "However, we are allowed to sit at a pub with a friend, are we not? Pull up a chair," she said, and DCI Williams looked at me questioningly.

"Has she gone off her meds or something?" he asked, and I laughed.

"No, no, nothing like that," Violet told him. "It is simply that a certain MI5 agent has had me followed for a number of days now, and I would rather they simply think this is a casual meal between coworkers."

"You know, the idea that British intelligence is following you is actually more realistic than you carrying on a normal human relationship," DCI Williams replied, grabbing a chair from the empty table next to us and sitting down. The waitress came by and he ordered a beer. "What is this really about, anyway?"

"There's a painting worth tens of millions of pounds hidden in the bathroom here."

"You have got to be joking," DCI Williams replied as Violet speared a piece of chicken onto her fork and ate it.

"I most certainly am not."

"The Milkmaid? It's here? That is the painting you're talking about, right?"

"Of course that's the painting," Violet scoffed. "And yes. It has been here the entire time. I thought perhaps you might enjoy taking the credit for its discovery."

"You know, some days I get phone calls from Violet and I think I need to find a new career. Then other days I get phone calls from her, and I get tempted to just grab her and plant a big fat kiss on her lips," DCI Williams told me.

"Please do not, a thank you would suffice," Violet said, and I laughed at them both.

"Well thank you," DCI Williams told her, shaking his head. "I still can't believe this is really happening. You seriously think the painting is in the bathroom here?"

"I do," Violet replied. "Come, we have spent enough time here now, let us go find us a stolen treasure."

The three of us went into the men's bathroom. It was simple and small – and thankfully empty – with just a sink and a toilet. There weren't exactly a million places to hide a priceless painting. However, it took

Violet less than a minute to fixate on a small vent near the ceiling.

"There," she said, pointing. I noticed that one of the three screws had actually fallen to the floor; it looked as though the vent had been moved since the last time this floor was cleaned.

DCI Williams' height came in handy; by standing on his tip-toes he could just reach the vent. He put on a pair of latex gloves, pulled a multi-tool from his pocket and worked on the other screws, and two minutes later, the vent had come off. Reaching into it, DCI Williams' eyes suddenly went wide as he pulled out a Harrods shopping bag.

I realized I wasn't breathing as DCI Williams pulled out a mailing tube about a foot and a half long.

"Let me," Violet ordered as she took latex gloves out of her purse and slipped them off. DCI Williams looked more than just a little bit relieved at being able to hand the painting off to Violet. Carefully, with precise movements, she pulled the painting from the tube. Holding it open, the three of us gazed onto one of the greatest masterpieces from a Dutch Master still in existence. My breath caught in my throat at the sheer beauty of it.

"I might not know much about art, but I know that's a bloody good painting," DCI Williams said. The colors and lighting were absolutely exquisite; it gave the painting a very realistic feel. The milkmaid in the painting poured the milk into a bowl, her frame lit by the sun pouring in through the window next to her.

It was one of the most incredible moments in my life, to be only inches away from something worth so much money.

"Now, we put it away," Violet said, rolling the painting back up and carefully putting it back in the tube. "DCI Williams, this is yours now. Do with it as you must. However, I ask that you please not release to the media that the painting has been found for at least a few hours."

"Wait," DCI Williams told Violet. "I need to know who stole it. I need some more details."

"Andrew Greenhouse stole it. He intended to pick it back up, along with his dinner, when he was certain Kevin Lin was dead, but he got caught in the blast instead. His fingerprints should be all over it; he was not wearing gloves when he was caught in the blast. However, I need a few hours to speak with him. I have proof he is a thief, but not a murderer. Not yet, at any rate."

"All right, how long do you need? I won't be able to give you more than twenty-four hours."

"That should be plenty; I will need only a few hours."

"Fine. I'll convince the higher-ups to hold off the press conference until tomorrow morning. Text me when we can go and arrest him."

"I knew there was a reason I called you and not one of your coworkers," Violet smiled.

"And boy do I ever appreciate it," DCI Williams replied. "The two of you should leave now; I'm going to call for a car to come pick me up just in case. This would be a bad day to be robbed on the underground."

Violet and I left, paid for the food, and made our way back into the street. Violet hailed us a cab, but instead of giving the cabbie our home address, she asked him to drive to St. Bartholomew's hospital.

"We're going to give Andrew Greenhouse a bit of a visit."

CHAPTER 20

As soon as we were in the cab I texted Brianne to ask what room Andrew Greenhouse was in. She texted me directions, and a room number, which I relayed back to Violet. Ward 4F, bed number thirty-two.

"Good," Violet replied, pulling a small laptop out of her purse and typing away on it furiously. By the time the taxi pulled up in front of the hospital, Violet still hadn't finished what she was doing, so we sat on a bench outside for a while. I looked over at her computer once or twice, but it was all gibberish to me; she was in a program that I didn't recognize, with words flying by on the screen.

Finally, about ten minutes later, Violet closed the lid in triumph.

"Good," she said. "We are ready."

"Why are we here?" I asked Violet. "Shouldn't the

cops be doing this sort of questioning? After all, even if you get Andrew Greenhouse to admit to the crimes, it's still he said-she said."

"You are correct, of course. Simply the recovery of the painting means that Greenhouse will be found guilty of the murders. I lied to DCI Williams: I do not want to find more evidence. With that painting, even the police and the Crown Prosecution Service will not be stupid enough to fail from here. And on top of that, there were likely fingerprints on the gas line, and I have also solved Jenny Lin's cipher; I know how LW refers to Andrew Greenhouse. But I want the whole story. I need to know exactly what happened, and exactly what the plan was. No one else will tell me. Follow my lead."

"Wait," I said. "Before we go in there… how did you figure out what the note meant? The LW leads back to Lin Wei, doesn't it?"

"Ah, but Jenny Lin was more clever than that. She had codes for nearly everything. For example, did you know the Mandarin word for 'milkmaid' is *jǐ nǎi nǚgōng*?"

I shook my head. "No, of course I didn't know that."

"And that the word for 'green' is *lùsè*? And the word for house is *wū*?"

"Ahhhh!" I exclaimed. "That's what the LW was for? Green House?"

"*Exactement*," Violet said, nodding. "It was not a difficult code to crack once I realized she was simply translating into Mandarin, but using the Roman alphabet."

I shook my head, completely impressed with Violet's problem-solving abilities as we made our way through the front doors of the hospital.

As soon as we made our way inside, immediately a flood of memories came rushing back to me. White walls and off-white tiles. That familiar smell. People rushing around. The sounds of worried families mingled with the efficient medical speak of the professionals trying to assuage their fears. It was like being punched in the stomach, in a way. The hospital was where some of my best memories were made. It was also where I woke up after the car crash. Where I learned that I was now a patient, instead of a doctor. It was where I learned I was never going to be a doctor.

"Cassie? Are you all right?" Violet asked in a surprisingly caring voice. I snapped out of my almost hypnotic state.

"What? Uh, yeah, I'm ok. Just… memories, you know?"

Violet looked at me with concern. "Are you sure you are up to doing this? If you would like, you can stay outside. I can take care of the interview myself, and you do not have to be in this hospital."

"No. No, it's ok," I said, shaking my head. The last thing I wanted was for being inside a hospital to become a trigger that reminded me of the worst time in my life. No,

I was going to continue on. I followed Violet to the reception desk, where a friendly, but overworked-looking woman wearing scrubs looked up at her with a wan smile.

"Can I help you?"

"Yes, we are here to visit a friend, Natalie Juneau, in Ward 4F please," Violet said.

The nurse typed something into the computer quickly, then nodded.

"Just take that lift over there please," she said, motioning to our left. Violet thanked her and made our way to the elevator. No matter what, I couldn't get that sinking feeling out of the pit of my stomach. This was my first time back in a hospital since I'd been discharged; my follow up appointments and physiotherapy had all taken place at a small clinic in San Francisco. I was not handling this well.

"It will get better," Violet said to me softly, giving my hand a quick squeeze, as we went up the elevator. I had to admit; I was touched. For all of her quirkiness, she noticed that I wasn't comfortable here, and she was actually helping.

When we got off the elevator we found ourselves at ward reception.

"Hello, we're here to see Natalie Juneau please," Violet said softly to the nurse at the station.

"Sign in here please," the lady said, and Violet signed the form. I noticed she used a false name, so I did as well. I was now Caroline Smith. It certainly wasn't the most creative name ever, but for the spur of the moment I didn't think it was too bad.

"She's in bed thirty-three, at the end of the ward, thank you," the nurse said as I handed her back the clipboard. We thanked her and made our way that way, but at the last second Violet quickly slipped into the room labeled *bed 32* instead.

Andrew Greenhouse had been given a private room; the hospital bed was in the center of it, a bathroom against the far wall. His heart rate monitor beeped steadily at around sixty BPM; he was obviously asleep. On the other side of the heart rate monitor was a crash cart and his IV hook-ups. When Violet closed the door behind her, he opened an eye.

"Who are you?" he asked. His voice was weak; it was obvious he hadn't done much speaking over the last few days.

"My name is Violet Despuis, and I know you killed the Lin children," Violet said.

"I don't know what you're talking about," Greenhouse replied, his voice stronger now.

"I also found the painting you stashed in the vent of the gent's at The Antelope."

That definitely got Greenhouse's attention. His eyes widened.

"How…" he asked, his voice trailing off.

"The how is not important right now. What is important is that you answer my questions. It is the only way you will get your painting back."

Greenhouse's eyes darted from Violet, to me, and back to Violet. He was obviously trying to make a decision here.

"How do I know you have the painting?" he asked.

"Well for one thing, I told you where you hid it," Violet said. "But if you need more proof," she continued, pulling a mailing tube that looked identical to the one we'd found in the bathroom out of her purse. I struggled not to look shocked. She had given that to DCI Williams. Surely, she had. Then it hit me: this one was a fake. Of course Violet would have thought to bring a fake.

"Give it to me," Greenhouse ordered, but Violet shook her head. "No. I am not interested in handing you over to the police, but I want answers. You tell me what I want to know, I give you back the painting."

Greenhouse snarled at her, but leaned back in his bed.

"How do I know you're not just going to take the painting to the police anyway?"

"You do not know that I won't. However, I can tell you that by refusing to answer my questions, you have absolutely zero chance of getting your painting back."

Greenhouse seemed to ponder the question for a little bit.

"Fine," he finally responded.

"Why did you kill the Lin kids?"

"I needed to ruin Lin Wei's smuggling operation.

With the kids gone, his whole method goes up in smoke."

"Why did you want to ruin his operation though?" I asked.

"He was ripping me off. I was getting him information on paintings worth stealing. He was paying me a commission based on the hot value of those paintings. Then I find out that he's making high-quality imitations of all the paintings—making three, five, sometimes six times the value of the painting, and sending the originals to his family in China for safekeeping. I decided to take The Milkmaid as back pay."

"How did you find out he was ripping you off?"

"I'm not an idiot. I have a contact apart from Lin Wei in the Bamboo Revolution. The contact told me what Lin Wei was doing."

Violet nodded. "So you effectively took his last, most valuable painting, then killed his entire smuggling operation as revenge for him not paying you what you thought you deserved?"

"Exactly. Now give me my painting."

"Fine," Violet said. She gave Greenhouse the mailing tube, and he relaxed visibly. He leaned back in his bed. "I got away with it, too. The police haven't even come to visit me, except to ask if I'd seen anything that night before the explosion. I told them about a Chinese looking man running from the scene a minute or so before the explosion, that should get them off my back permanently. They have no idea it was me. How the hell did you figure it out?"

"All of the paintings Lin Wei stole were insured by your company. Once I discovered what the Lin twins were doing, and found Jenny Lin's list of paintings, it was easy to put two and two together."

"I still don't see how you found the painting."

"You had to store it somewhere, it wasn't found on you when you were taken to the hospital, so it had to be nearby."

Andrew Greenhouse shook his head. "You're better than the police, I have to give you that."

"Of course I am," Violet replied. Suddenly, however, Greenhouse leapt out of the bed and grabbed Violet in a chokehold. She was only a foot or so away from his bed, and didn't have a chance to react. Violet kicked out multiple times, but I quickly remembered what Lin Wei had said: his contact was an expert in Kung Fu. Violet was strong, and she was a skilled fighter, but I wasn't sure she stood a chance against someone like that.

Suddenly, all of my medical training kicked in automatically. I darted over to the crash cart and opened the top drawer. Grabbing the pre-loaded syringe full of suxamethonium chloride I ran over to where Greenhouse was still choking Violet. She was struggling to breathe; I knew I had to act fast. I wasn't in any sort of condition to fight a grown man, but I knew he couldn't take us both on at once.

I had once sedated a schizophrenic who thought we were the CIA coming to kill him. I'd also had to sedate a two-hundred and fifty pound wife-beater who'd been shot by his wife's best friend in her defense, who was trying to escape the hospital so he could kill her. This was nothing.

Honing in on the IV, I jammed the syringe in and pressed, hard.

"What the hell did you just put into me?" Greenhouse asked between clenched teeth. Violet was struggling less and less now; only a few more seconds and I knew she'd be unconscious.

However, only seconds later, the sux—as it's commonly referred to by medical professionals—kicked in and Greenhouse fell to the floor, completely sedated.

Violet gasped for air, clutching at her throat. "Well, Andrew Greenhouse will now truly be spending the rest of his life in jail; on top of the theft and two murders the police can add attempted murder to the charges. Thank you, Cassie. I knew it was a good idea to bring you."

"It turns out I still remember what drugs are in a crash cart," I replied, looking at the unconscious body on the ground. Violet took out her phone and sent a text; I imagined DCI Williams would be on his way to arrest Greenhouse soon.

"Well I, for one, am happy that your medical knowledge came in handy for more than simply identifying Jenny Lin's cause of death for me."

"Me too. You're crazy, but your cases are certainly interesting."

"How long will the sedative last?" Violet asked, and I shrugged.

"Probably about fifteen, twenty minutes. The recommended dose is one to one and a half ml per kilo, and I didn't exactly check his weight or how much was in the vial before I stuck it in him. If I dosed him properly, he'd be awake in ten, but I suspect I put in a bit more than I had to. Don't worry, there should be another sedative in there if we need it."

"Good," Violet said. "I do not need a repeat of that experience."

"Who knew even Violet Despuis has a weakness?" I joked.

"It was not that *I* was weak," Violet said. "He was simply a skilled fighter, and I expected him to be weaker than he was after his stay in hospital."

"Ah," I said, trying to hide the smile on my face. Violet was completely incapable of admitting any sort of fault.

"Although," she said, "I probably should have remembered Lin Wei mentioning that his contact was skilled in the art of Kung Fu. That was—how do you say—very sloppy of me."

"I think you might need to sit down, obviously the flow of oxygen to your brain is still constricted if you admitted you made a mistake," I told Violet, who laughed.

"You joke, but I think I will sit," she said. As soon as she said it, I was up on my feet. I didn't have a stethoscope so I took her pulse manually. Seventy beats per minute. A little bit high for Violet, but not too bad at all considering someone had tried to kill her a moment ago.

She acquiesced as I moved her neck around, making sure there was no damage.

"I'm fine," she insisted as I poked and prodded her.

"I'll be the judge of that," I said, but quickly realized that she was correct. Considering what she'd just been through, Violet was in great shape.

"I thought you gave the painting to DCI Williams," I said when I eventually decided Violet wasn't in any immediate danger.

"I did," she replied. "I simply went and bought a similar tube. It does have a Milkmaid in it, but it is not real."

"Wouldn't Andrew Greenhouse have immediately known it was a fake?"

Violet smiled. "Ah, but no. You do remember the man we met at the Museum of Natural History?"

"Edward? The skinny geologist who likes rocks and paintings?"

"Yes, him. He is in fact one of the most skilled art forgers in the country. He had the fake made for me after my visit, in case I was in need of it. He warned me that the work was very rushed, but it would have easily passed muster with all but the most experienced art historian."

I didn't even know what to say. I'd had no idea that the man working with the rocks at the museum was actually an art forger. Violet ran in strange, strange circles.

Just then DCI Williams entered the room.

"We were waiting outside for your text; ready to come in whenever," he said as he saw the unconscious Greenhouse on the floor. "Is everything all right?"

"You can add two counts of murder and one count of attempted murder to the charges," Violet told him. "I will warn you though: MI5 won't be happy."

"That stuff is for my bosses to hash out," DCI Williams replied. "I'm sure they'll take the flak from the intelligence services in exchange for getting the glory of solving this case."

"Agent Tompkins isn't going to be happy," I said to Violet.

"Agent Tompkins is never happy," she replied with a smile.

CHAPTER 21

The next twenty-four hours or so went by in a blur. First of all, Violet and I both had to go to the police station to get our official statements taken by DCI Williams when it came to the attack on Violet.

After spending three hours in the police station, I wanted nothing more than to go home, collapse into bed, and sleep for at least twelve hours, but Biscuit had other ideas. He meowed at me when I returned, complaining that I'd been neglecting his regular walks for the last few days.

"All right little guy," I told him, grabbing his leash and harness. "Let's go for a walk, then I'm ordering Chinese food and scarfing it down as fast as I can before passing out." That certainly sounded like a good plan to me.

Biscuit happily jumped down off the chair he was standing on and trotted toward the door, patiently waiting for me to put the harness on him, and then happily bounding outside, scaring a pigeon standing on the sidewalk outside my suite.

We made our way to Kensington Gardens, where I ran into Linda, walking Kiki, looking a little bit depressed.

"Hey, what's wrong?" I asked her when I saw her. Linda sighed.

"Just having one of those days, you know? I was on a date with Aaron last night, and I mentioned my sister, and he got noticeably uncomfortable. I'm sure he's lying to me, you know?"

I nodded. "I do know, actually. And I think I can possibly put your mind at ease."

"Oh I told you not to bother your friend with my dumb problems," Linda told me.

"I didn't! I swear. I actually ended up looking into it a bit myself."

With that, I told Linda what I'd found out, that Aaron's sister was in jail.

"Oh," Linda said when I finally finished. She walked away from me for a minute, processing the information I told her, then turned back to me. "You know, that actually makes a lot of sense," she said. "I mean, yeah, I kind of wish he told me, but at the same time I can also understand him not wanting to. No one wants to have to admit to someone they've dated like three times that their sister's in jail, you know?"

"Yeah," I replied. "That was what I thought as well when I found out. I mean sure, he could have just told you he had a sister and then not said anything about her, but he probably didn't want to lie to you if you started asking questions about her, so thought ignoring her existence completely would be the right way to go."

Linda smiled at me. "This actually made me feel a lot better, thanks Cassie."

"No problem," I replied, feeling a flush of warmth crawl up me. I hadn't really helped someone like this in almost a year now. It brought back the memories of being able to tell someone that their cancer was now in remission after they had gone through chemotherapy. Of taking off a cast and telling someone they could use their arm normally again. Of reassuring a worried parent that their child was cured of meningitis and was going to be fine.

For the first time in nearly a year, I felt *needed*. And it felt good. As I left the park with Biscuit and headed home, I started thinking of other ways I could go back to helping people. I was thinking about the future again. That was a good sign, right?

* * *

THE NEXT DAY Violet and I were called back into the

police station to answer some more questions about exactly how Andrew Greenhouse had committed the crimes. This mainly involved Violet answering the questions, and me sitting next to her silently.

We were just leaving when Agent Tompkins made his presence known. He had ditched his two other men in black and now stormed over to where Violet and I were leaving, DCI Williams holding the door open for us. He was practically frothing at the mouth.

"You!" he spat. "I told you to stay the hell away from my case. Now I find you handed the murderer to the Met police. You're a disgrace to England; I should have you deported."

"I was not looking into the murder case. I looked into the theft of a high value painting. The fact that it led directly to the murderer you weren't able to find before me is not my fault. Besides, I did not arrest anyone. As you are well aware, that is the police's job."

"I don't care who gets the credit. I know it was you. You steamrolled me, and now I'm going to get chewed out by my boss for failing to catch the murderer."

"Well, if you were better at your job, perhaps that would not have happened. By the way, I recommend that you drop the mistress. I already told you that your wife is not happy with you, so I suspect that she knows. I would beg for her forgiveness if you value your marriage."

"How... you little... URGH!" Tompkins finally cried

out. He sounded like an angry elephant, and I struggled not to laugh. At this point most of the other cops in the room had realized there was drama happening, and had all stopped what they were doing to see what was going to happen.

"You'll be hearing from my superior," Tompkins said, taking a threatening step toward Violet. I saw her smile as he came toward her, but DCI Williams stepped between them before anything else could happen.

"All right, agent. I know you've got a beef with Miss Despuis, but this is not the place for that. I must politely ask you to leave the station now."

"Oh you're just defending her because you tosspots stole my case and took all the glory," Tompkins muttered to DCI Williams, but he did turn around and leave.

I looked around the room and noticed Jake standing off to one side. As soon as I saw him my heart skipped a beat and I felt a flush come to my face. It was like I was back in elementary school again, and I scolded myself at my own reaction. However, I found myself gravitating toward him, as though my body was acting completely independently of my brain.

"Hey," he said to me with a smile. "I see you've been busy."

"Yeah, but things are definitely wrapping up," I said, trying to sound cool and casual. "Thankfully. Have you ever been held at gunpoint by a bunch of Chinese gangsters?"

"I can't say I have," Jake said, looking surprised.

"I wish I could say the same," I replied, and Jake laughed.

"Why don't you tell me about it over dinner?" he asked. "It sounds like you've had quite an adventure."

"Sure," I smiled. "I thought being held at knifepoint by a woman who had killed four people was the most exciting my life was ever going to get, but it turned out I was wrong. How about you? How are things going?"

"Luckily, all the criminals I have to deal with are already dead. I haven't been held at gunpoint recently; the worst thing that's happened to me this week was I had to open up a man who died of sepsis. That didn't smell great. But that's also not excellent dinner conversation, so we'll stick to your story. How does tomorrow night sound?"

"Tomorrow night sounds great," I told Jake with a smile. My stomach fluttered at the thought. A real date! I'd gone on a bit of an accidental half-date with Jake a little while ago, but this was a real, honest-to-God, date with a boy. And a very hot boy at that. Maybe I could even splurge on a new dress for the occasion. Things were definitely looking up.

* * *

Book 3: Cassie's adventures continue in Whacked in Whitechapel. When a nurse is found murdered in a hospital, Cassie thinks it's just going to be a standard case. She never expects to find herself embroiled in a middle of a terrorist plot!

Click or tap here now to read Whacked in Whitechapel

ALSO BY SAMANTHA SILVER

Thank you so much for reading! If you enjoyed Bombing in Belgravia please help other readers find this book so they can enjoy it, too.

- Write a review on Amazon
- Sign up for my newsletter here to be the first to find out about new releases: http://www.samanthasilverwrites.com/newsletter
- Check out the next book in this series, Whacked in Whitechapel, by clicking here: http://www.samanthasilverwrites.com/whackedinwhitechapel

You can also check out any of the other series I write by clicking the links below:

Non-Paranormal Cozy Mysteries

Cassie Coburn Mysteries

Ruby Bay Mysteries

Paranormal Cozy Mysteries

Western Woods Mysteries

Pacific North Witches Mysteries

Pacific Cove Mysteries

Willow Bay Witches Mysteries

Magical Bookshop Mysteries

California Witching Mysteries

ABOUT THE AUTHOR

Samantha Silver lives in British Columbia, Canada, along with her husband and a little old doggie named Terra. She loves animals, skiing and of course, writing cozy mysteries.

You can connect with Samantha online here:
    Facebook
    Email

Made in the USA
Monee, IL
10 April 2025

15532926R00121